YOU'RE WELCOME, UNIVERSE

WHITNEY GARDNER

Alfred A. Knopf
New York

THIS IS A BORZOI BOOK PUBLISHED BY ALFRED A. KNOPF

All rights reserved. Published in the United States by
Alfred A. Knopf, an imprint of Random House Children's Books,
a division of Penguin Random House LLC, New York.

Knopf, Borzoi Books, and the colophon are registered trademarks of
Penguin Random House LLC.

Visit us on the Web! randomhouseteens.com

Educators and librarians, for a variety of teaching tools,
visit us at RHTeachersLibrarians.com

Library of Congress Cataloging-in-Publication Data is available upon request.

ISBN 978-0-399-55141-3 (trade) | ISBN 978-0-399-55142-0 (lib. bdg.) |
ISBN 978-0-399-55143-7 (ebook)

The text of this book is set in 12-point Apollo MT.

Printed in the United States of America
March 2017

10 9 8 7 6 5 4 3 2 1

First Edition

For all the girls looking to
leave their mark on the world

Six stencils in and it's gone. Okay, the tag vanished by Stencil Number Two, but I have a point to prove. I'm not covering up your scribbled slur with just anything. I'm *making art* here. I'm creating. I'm on fire.

I've never thrown up such an intense piece—I was worried I wouldn't be able to pull it off in time. My arm flies across the wall, pink paint striping across the last stencil. It looks like it's going to work out. I chuckle to myself. This is what it's all been for, the hours of paint-pen practice, filling up every inch of every sketchbook with tags and words and pictures. All my hard work has paid off, and it's all up here on the wall.

I know I shouldn't be tagging the school. *I know that*. But I wasn't the first, and that mess had to go. Jordyn told the principal that someone tagged the gym, she had to. The vandal singled her out, and word gets around real quick at Kingston School for the Deaf. But three weeks went by, and "Jordyns a SLUT" was still there on the back of the gym for all to see. And good ole Principal Howard hadn't done a damn thing.

No one gets to call my best friend a slut, especially not up on a wall, not on my turf. She asked for help, and I took matters into my own paint-stained hands. I designed a killer piece, cut out the stencils, shook up the cans, and got to work.

I'm getting away with it. I'm about to get up. On my way

to becoming an all-city queen of street art. I rip down the last stencil, take a step back, and admire my work. It's killer. You're welcome, Universe. I check over both of my shoulders again, eyes on constant watch. I can't rely on my ears, so my eyes work overtime. It's nice and dark. I pretend I'm nothing but a shadow.

I'm so proud I just can't help myself and I text Jordyn a picture of the new mural on my way back home.

(λ_入)

"**Y**ou don't have any proof!" I snap at our principal.

"Don't lie to me, Julia. You'll only make it worse." His hands are big, with stubby fingers. He might be hearing, but he signs perfectly. He has to, or he never would have gotten the job.

"I'm not lying! You can't say it was me." I know there are no cameras on that side of Kingston. I know there won't be any footage to review.

"I have all the proof I need. Look at your hands!"

I'm so stupid. I was being lazy. I'm going to need to buy gloves. Lots and lots of gloves.

"This was from art class." I sign as fast as I can before dropping my hands out of view and into my lap.

"I'm going to give you one more chance to tell the truth, Miss Prasad." Mr. Howard seems more agitated than angry. He keeps sighing, looking at me with droopy, tired eyes.

"I don't know what to tell you. Sorry." *Let me go already, you've got nothing.* He stares at me, waiting for a better answer. I'm not giving it to him. I'm not confessing to anything, as much as I want to take credit for it. He hangs his head and pinches the bridge of his nose.

"Well, what can you tell me about this?"

My heart shakes up in my chest like a paint can as he produces a cell phone from his desk drawer, the case dotted

3

with red cherries. It's Jordyn's. He slides it across the desk like some detective on *Law & Order*.

I don't want to look. I don't need to. I know what's about to happen. And I know without looking that Jordyn, my best friend in the universe, sold me out. *How could she?*

"The paint on your hands, the picture on her phone. You can't tell me you didn't do it."

"Fine. But I was covering up—"

"That's not your job."

"Well, whose job is it? Because that nasty graffiti was up there forever."

"Not *your* job. We had someone scheduled to take care of it."

"But mine is art!"

"That's not art, it's vandalism. I'm worried about you; you're not exactly showing any remorse here," he lectures. My face flushes hot with rage. He's not worried about me, he's relieved he has someone to pin it on. I wonder if the slut-shaming toy-tagger got the fifth degree, too. I doubt it.

"I don't understand what the big deal is! I didn't hurt anyone. I didn't destroy anything. I've tagged the girls' room dozens of times. No one cared then—"

"You *what*?!" His face is turning as red as mine.

"So now, when I try to make something worthwhile, *art* even, you're up in arms, calling me a vandal?" Just tell me how much detention I have so we can all move on with our lives, and I can X-Acto–cut Jordyn out of mine. I wonder how long she had to sit here before stabbing me in the back. She's spineless, so she's always asked me to break the rules for her. Which I've done plenty of times, because I thought we were a team. I bet all Mr. Howard had to do was ask, and she rolled right over like a David Hockney dachshund. The light

4

by Mr. Howard's door flashes, indicating first period is about to begin. All my anger fizzles away and I just feel weak, depleted at the thought of Jordyn heading off to her first class, no worries, all smiles, while I get interrogated.

Mr. Howard stands up and walks to his office door without saying a word. He opens it and my stomach flips; all my bravado turns bashful as he ushers my mothers into the room. It's one thing to piss off the principal. I can barely look at my parents as he tells them I'm expelled.

It's silent.

Who am I kidding? It's always silent, but this—I can *feel* it. Like for the first time, I know what the word really means. It pounds in my head. Silence is the loudest sound. Ma doesn't scowl in the rearview. Mee doesn't sign a word.

I messed up. It was beautiful. Not a masterpiece but, I don't know, close? Didn't matter, got caught. Shouldn't have done it on school property and definitely shouldn't have texted anyone evidence; those were toy mistakes and I knew better. I stood up for Jordyn, tried to save her dignity. She cried and cried the day we discovered it. And when it looked like the school wasn't going to help her, I did. I helped her, and she ratted me out—I just don't understand. I get expelled and Jordyn gets what? Nothing.

The expulsion was an overreaction, if you ask me. But that was the "final straw" and "the school won't be responsible" for whatever "mayhem" (really?) I cause next. My first real piece and I'm expelled. And now I need a new tag. Go ahead, call me a vandal, say I'm some sort of delinquent, it isn't going to insult me. It's not going to stop me. Please. *This is what I live for.*

Silence. I stare at the backs of my parents' heads, waiting for one of them to start in on me. Waiting for Mee's pointer finger to fly to her chin with that grimace she saves for special occasions.

Disappointed.

It never comes, so I kick off my shoes and rush upstairs as soon as we're home. If they're not talking yet, I'm not going to be the first. I crash-land onto my bed face-first and grip the quilt in clenched fists. I pound the mattress. *What's! Wrong! With! Her?!* Who would do something like that? She was the only real friend I had, the only one who knew me and my whole paint-splattered story. It eats at me, worming its way through my stomach and up to my brain. Neither organ can make any sense of it.

My phone vibrates in my pocket, and I'm hoping Jordyn has a damn good explanation for what she did to me. Because only one person I know would be texting me right now.

JORDYN: Srry :(

JULIA: щ(°Д°щ)
That's it?

JORDYN: They were gonna call the cops. On
meeee!

JULIA: ¬_¬

JULIA: No. They weren't.

JORDYN: Mayb.

JULIA: They kicked *me* out!

JORDYN: I didnt think they would really do it.

JULIA: WHY

JORDYN: Idk. I mean u did break the law and stuff.

JULIA: Standing up for you!

JORDYN: U didn't have to. I didnt ask u.

JULIA: Are you kidding me?!?!

JORDYN: It's not like u care abt getting in trouble.

JORDYN: I did u a favor. Ur gonna be famous now.

JORDYN: Don't be so mad.

I stuff my phone under my pillow. I don't care what else she has to say. Nothing can make up for what's already been done. Nothing.

(」 °口°)」

I love gray days. Every tree, building, telephone pole high-lighted against the gesso-colored sky. This past week has been especially overcast and it's a relief. I thought getting registered at a new school would take at least a month, that I would get to stay out of the educational system for a while. But with both of my moms at the helm, it only took four days. Now, three weeks in at Finley, the spotlight hasn't grown any dimmer. I welcome the clouds. Bring on the fog.

It's getting to be that time of year when it's still dark in the morning and the roads are empty. The drive to Fin-ley is one of the few things I don't hate about the transfer. You would think the forty minutes it takes to commute from Queens Village would suck, but I love driving. Gives me time to think. I drive through the 'burbs of Greenlawn with the tree-lined sidewalks and traffic lights reflecting in the wet road. The leaves aren't turning yet, but they're about to. I spot a red leaf here and there, pilot lights to the season. Just me and my car, Lee.

Good ole Lee. I bought her off of Craigslist this summer for twelve hundred bucks, a 1994 Oldsmobile. She's older than I am, but she's got some moves left. When I got her, she was this horrible maroon color. Now she's perfect: black and white, with flecks of color here and there.

Krasner meets Basquiat. That's Lee. She's the only real friend I have left, the only one who's never let me down.

I fish through my bag on the passenger seat, getting my morning ritual started en route. Pull out a can of Red Bull, hold it between my thighs (I'm an expert at driving one-handed), and crack it open. I hate coffee. It's either bitter or sour or chalky, not to mention the bad breath. Red Bull isn't the most delicious morning elixir, but a girl's gotta get a jolt from something.

Pulling into the parking lot of my new hellscape, I look for a spot up front in case I need to make a quick getaway. I haven't actually tried escaping from school yet, but you never know. Doesn't matter that the overly accommodating administrators reserved a spot for me next to the front doors. I refuse to park there. I can walk. Don't baby me.

I don't get the best spot this morning, but it's not a gym day, so I probably won't feel the need to flee. I reach to put Lee into Park when—*SLAM!*—she lurches forward and my seat belt digs into my chest. I swivel around in my seat and look out the rear window.

Kyle Fucking Stokers.

He tried to park in my spot, not noticing that my car was already there. What a tool. He's one of those people who's unaware of anyone or anything else in his vicinity. Bow down to him, the only person on earth who truly matters. So of course this whole ordeal is about to be blamed on me. Doesn't matter that I was already parked, minding my own business. I exist, therefore I am at fault.

I get out, not bothering to put on my shoes. My socks are getting damp as I walk around on the wet pavement. Lee's bumper is okay, no real harm done. Tough bird. Some of my paint job has come away, but the maroon showing through isn't a tragedy. I'm the only person who would even notice. Before I can get a closer look, there's hands on my shoulders and Kyle spins me around to face him. He's yelling.

"What—-—-——-parking here?!"

There's always a moment when one of these kids asks me a question and I have to figure out if speaking is worth the risk.

I cross my arms.

"You—--aint—my bum—r!" he rages. It's not easy to lip-read when people are yelling at you. Despite what the distorted-face yeller might actually think.

I stare back at Kyle. He probably spent more time on his dusty blond hair this morning than I ever spend on mine. He has great eyebrows, but that's beside the point.

"Well?" He gestures to his car again and again, trying to drive his point home.

Walking over to his slick silver car, I spit on my sleeve. *I* should be yelling at *him*. I should scream and say, "You ran into ME, dipshit!" Honestly? He's not worth it. I buff off the paint and gesture at the spot. *All better.* I raise my eyebrows and smile. He doesn't catch the sarcasm.

"Bitches shouldn't drive," he says slowly, deliberately. I catch every word. He turns and walks toward the school. I imagine throwing my keys at him, chasing him down, kicking his shins until he's on the ground. I slam my fists into his chest over and over and—

There's a tap on my shoulder and I snap to. Kyle disappears into school through the double doors.

"Julia! Where are your shoes?" Casey signs. She's looking at me like I'm crazy, not a hair out of place in her perfectly cut chin-length bob. Her eyes behind her black-framed glasses are magnified to a ridiculous size, like something out of a Margaret Keane painting. I point over to Lee.

"One minute," I reply. "See you in history." I shoo her away from me, because the last thing I need is Casey thinking she can solve all my problems *outside* of class, too.

I get back in the car and peel off my socks. Great. Now I'm going to end up with blisters. Mee bought me new Doc Martens before the transfer. She winked when she gave them to me—a signal she reserves for when something is to be kept just between us. Ma would kill her if she knew Mee was buying me gifts now. Rightfully so; I know I don't deserve them. But they make me smile. They're yellow, my favorite color. Problem is, they're impossible to break in and twice as impossible to drive in, so I drive in my socks and put the boots on before school. I squeeze my size 10 feet in and lace them up loosely.

I reach into the backseat to grab my hoodie, but the one I

pull out isn't mine. It's Jordyn's, all purple and pilly. It even smells like her. How long has it been in here? Sand spills out of the folds, and I remember that day on Coney Island when we shared a spicy mango on a stick. Like we always did. Like we never will again. Not any time soon. I shove it under the passenger seat. I can't stand to look at it right now.

I need my own hoodie, my trusty black-faded-gray-with-age armor. The sleeves and hem flecked with rainbows of spray paint. This is what I wear when I go out and tag stuff. I yank the zipper up to my chin, and I'm protected. The hood falls over my two loose black buns, down over my ears. I take my bag, open my second Red Bull, and drink it, heading toward the big blue building.

At first I thought transferring to Finley wouldn't be a big deal. School is school; I hated it at Kingston, I'd hate it at Finley. I mean, Jordyn is always going out with hearies and they seem fine, but it's not like I'm looking to make friends. I don't have time for that shit anymore. Not after Jordyn showed me what she's really made of. No one here would even notice me, right?

Casey took care of that right quick. Having an interpreter in every class is like having a giant neon sign hanging around your neck, blinking: *Freak Freak Freak*. I've been here three weeks and people are still confused about how it all works. It's not hard: teacher talks, interpreter signs, I understand. They act like Casey's conjuring black magic, waving her arms around, when really she's only blathering on about tariffs or decimal places.

I toss the empty Red Bull into the recycling bin and head for my locker. Mine is stuck in the freshman hall, even though I'm a junior, because it's one of the few left over from the start of the year. I open it up and all of a sudden I feel lighter. I take a certain pride in every tag, and I've done a good job claiming my space here. I know I shouldn't have tagged the inside of the door, but I couldn't help myself. A new color for every week, my tag, my sign: *HERE*.

(⊙_⊙)

U.S. History isn't so bad because no one is awake yet, not even Mr. Clarke. It's the only class I'm glad to have Casey around for, because watching his wrinkly old-man lips collect foamy spittle in their corners makes me want to hurl.

Casey always has her nails painted some fun color. It's a huge interpreter no-no, but I won't report her; it's easier on the eyes than old-man spit-mouth.

"You found your shoes!" she signs, hitting her fists together.

"Yay." I wave my hands next to my deadpan face.

Casey stands up and I take the seat from her. She always gets to class early to "prep," which looks a lot like sucking up to the teachers. I think she's trying to prove her worth by getting me better grades. Ma hired her specifically; Casey shadowed her last year for some sort of college credit. Sometimes I wonder if Ma chose Casey so she could spy on me. Fresh out of terp school and shining with enthusiasm after finding her calling, Casey doesn't know why I was expelled, but she's on a mission to "improve my quality of life." I'm sure she goes home and talks to whatever friends she has about how brave I am. I didn't choose to be deaf. I have no idea why it makes me brave.

The underpass is what makes me brave. I don't know when I'll have time to go out there, but it had better be soon. I've had plans for it ever since I laid my eyeballs on it. I'm going crazy sitting around the house at night, scrolling through the Stencil Bomb forums until I pass out. My life has to be about more than the Refresh button. After my Kingston piece, with all the risk and the rush, painting in the basement isn't really cutting it anymore. I want to make art that makes my heart race. Art that demands to be felt, even if that feeling is terror.

"You have your homework?" Casey asks. *She* asks, not Mr. Clarke. It's not *her* job to ask. I've told her this before. The only thing she's supposed to do is interpret for the teachers and me—not police my homework, or scold me for doing poorly on a test. I'm about to lay into her again when I feel the girl sitting behind me staring. I take the worksheet out of my bag and hand it to Casey. At least I did my homework this time.

The girl behind me taps my shoulder. She's got glossy blond bouncing bangs and long feather earrings. I don't think she owns any jeans; I've only ever seen her in yoga pants. Thankfully not the kind you can see through, but she does seem to own a pair in every possible color. And animal print.

"Look, I go a new slines!"

I'm not very good at lip-reading to begin with, and that wad of gum she's gnawing on isn't making it any easier. I'm sure I look puzzled when she starts signing. "Friend. Family. I love you."

Ah, she knows the same signs every other hearing kindergartner learns. She's looking for her gold star, no doubt. I beam at her, and sign back happily, "Bitch. You don't. Know me." She gives me a thumbs-up and goes back to her work.

. . .

"Why did you do that?" Casey asks as we make our way down the hall after class.

"What?"

"Why did you say that to her?"

"Who, Yoga Pants? She couldn't understand me. I wasn't starting anything." I wonder how many of the students who stop and stare at our conversation end up being late to their next class.

"She was trying to be nice!" Casey's eyebrows angle together in annoyance.

"Nice? What should I have said? 'Wow! You know three signs, I can see we're gonna be BFFs! Oh, the late-night chats and . . .'"

"Come on! You're never going to make friends if you don't lose the attitude."

"Who said I wanted to make friends? I think—"

There it is, a glimpse of red plaid flannel, and I'm off charging after it like a bull. Only when I'm tapping Mr. Katz on his shoulder do I realize I made a mistake leaving Casey behind.

"Julia? What's wrong?" Mr. Katz asks me. I try signing first.

"Please." I rub my palm on my chest. He doesn't understand me. I switch my hands up to look like I'm begging. I plead with my eyes. I squeeze my interlocked fingers and suck air in through my teeth.

"My class is full. I'm sorry. Truly." Mr. Katz's brown eyes show real regret. He moves to leave, but I dash in front of him and open my bag. A few other students have stopped to watch me play my version of charades. I couldn't care less. I pull out my sketchbook (not my Black Book, which is full of plans that aren't superlegal) and put it in his hands.

"Please," I sign again. "I can't go a whole quarter with no art classes!" I don't care if he doesn't know exactly what I'm saying—I'm sure he gets the gist. I've been asking to get into his advanced-art studio class since my first day at Finley.

He flips through my book and I bounce on the balls of my feet, watching his face intently for his reaction. Mr. Katz handles my sketchbook thoughtfully. Even though we're both pressed for time, he holds it in his hands like a baby bird, gingerly turning each page and considering its worth. Sometimes he smiles.

I *need* to be in Mr. Katz's class.

His focus is broken abruptly and he glances upward at the ceiling. It must be the bell. Great, I've made him late. He holds up a finger and takes a pen from his red flannel pocket. I wonder how many of those shirts he owns. I rarely see him wearing anything else. He carefully turns to the back page of my book and writes:

We'll see.

(¬‿¬)

I can feel Ma stomp her foot to get my attention before I leave the house. Should I make a run for it? She stomps again and I turn around.

"Your bag." She doesn't ask to see it, she *demands*, and I fork it over. Most moms search for drugs and skimpy clothes and stuff. Mine is looking for paint pens and spray cans.

Ma and I look nothing alike. She's fair with green eyes; Mee calls her an Irish gem (try not to gag). I'm the spitting image of Mee: oil-black hair, big feet, brown skin. I'm her little jewel of India. Get it? *Jewel, Jewel-ia, Julia* (more gagging, I know).

I love watching Ma's hands when she signs. Normally, you just watch someone's face while they're signing. But I can't keep my eyes off Ma's hands. I know it doesn't make any sense, seeing as she's not my bio-mom, but our hands are very similar. Sometimes when she's talking to me it's like I'm watching my own in the mirror. Except the mirror hands have a perfect manicure and wedding band and mine are— were—always covered in paint and Sharpie ink.

"I wish I didn't have to do this." She holds out my backpack, inspection complete.

"So don't." I zip it up and sling it over my shoulders.

"I want you back home by ten thirty, no messing around after work." More demands. One wave and I'm out the door.

The inspections haven't let up. Ma went through Lee the day of my expulsion and pretty much gutted the car of anything I could make a mark with. I'll admit I wasn't being careful. That's the problem when your own personal contraband comes in the form of *basically* legal art supplies. I never thought I would have to stash anything. I was such a freaking toy. I've had to step my game *way* up since then. I'm not the kind of person to make the same mistakes over and over again.

I feel my phone vibrate in my pocket: Jordyn, no doubt, looking to see where I'm at. She's so oblivious. She should have deleted my number the second she got her phone back from the principal. After that pathetic attempt at an apology she still likes to send me vapid, meaningless texts even though I only ever text back the same thing:

JORDYN: Wrks boring without D.

JULIA: k

Jordyn and I both work at McDonald's four or five shifts a week, thanks to Kingston's job-placement program. When I got expelled, I thought I might get fired, too. I guess they figured a delinquent like me would need a job, especially a punishing one that involves standing over a fryer for hours.

Jordyn has a cochlear implant. That's how she gets along so well with all of her boyfriends, and with everyone else. It also means she gets a better job at Mickey D's. Not only does she work the registers, she's also a *beverage specialist,* making sure all the shakes and faux-Frappuccinos and sodas come out right. It's a stupid job, but it's better than fry girl. No one has to talk to the fry girl.

That's all I get to do. Fries go in, fries come out. Fries go in their little bags to go into bigger bags. Don't forget the salt. I almost got fired when I first got the job; the timer didn't have a light on it, and I might have burned a batch while I was distracted by Donovan's seven o'clock shadow.

Donovan Diaz. No one hates working at McDonald's more than Donovan. He has the worst job out of all of us: the drive-thru window. I can't quite imagine the stress of it, not fully, anyway. He stands in the window with his little headset on, grimacing at people who think they have to scream into the intercom. At least that's one thing I understand; Jordyn, too. People find out I'm deaf and think that yelling at me is the cure. I've seen Jordyn switch off her CI mid-conversation with that same pinched face. Rude, but less painful, I'm sure.

I have a front-row seat to all the drive-thru drama from my station. It's too bad Donovan faces away from me and I miss most of the details. I definitely stare too much. I've learned to read his body language as he leans on the window with those forearms of his—you know, the kind with perfectly smooth arm hairs—gesturing with his hands and stubby, chewed-up fingernails when he talks with customers, a slight bend in his knees. That's when I know he's on a good streak. The next time he turns around, he'll be smiling, a smile that has been known to pacify an enraged customer as soon as they see it shining through the window.

It's not like Donovan's ever done anything nice or cute for me. I don't know all that much about him, either. I don't know if he has any hobbies, or what his favorite movie is. I only know his work schedule and that he drives a 1997 purple Jetta. And he has wild black-blue hair that sticks straight up, like an Egon Schiele self-portrait.

There's just undeniably something about him. Maybe it's because he's never asked me stupid questions about my ears, or even cared that I can't hear him. We just exist in the same place at the same time and we're both fine.

He's hot, okay?

I'm not all that good at getting guys interested in me, let alone hearie guys. That's Jordyn. She gets whatever she wants, and she doesn't mind stepping on anyone to get it—and then flaunting it in their face.

Fries go in, fries come out. Fries go in, fries come out. Small, regular, large, extra-large. Fries go in, fries come out. Sweat drips down my back, my chest burning hot. I try not to scald my forearms when people slam into me, rushing between stations. Fries go in, fries come out. I am the siren call of McDonald's: smell the fries, you cannot resist. You want the fries. You need the fries. I hate the fries. I am the fries. Fries go in, fries come out.

After our shift I make myself a shake with extra Reese's Pieces mixed in. It's only about a billion degrees over the fryer, and all I want after work is an ice bath. The shake is the next best thing.

"I'm all hyped up! Wanna do something?" Jordyn flings her visor into her locker. All of her tight curly hair falls onto her shoulders.

"Seriously? I'm still on lockdown. Because of *you*." I

wouldn't go anyway. Treachery aside, work doesn't hype me up. It burns me out.

"Still? They painted over it. No one even remembers anymore."

My stomach turns over, a lump hardens in my throat. I figured they would patch over it, but to actually find out that no one remembers it? Needles at my skin. People have stopped talking about my grand departure already? I used six colors for that piece. It was a labor-intensive stencil job that I managed to get up in under twenty minutes. I thought the legend never dies, or some shit.

Jordyn takes forever to get her things together. She can't be that dense, that aloof. Asking me to hang out, like she never turned me in, like it wasn't a big deal. It was. It is! I used to be able to count on her. We had a deal, an understanding. I wouldn't judge the parade of boys that marched through her life, and she wouldn't judge my illicit afterschool activities. We were outcasts, and we leaned on each other. I thought we needed each other. Now, I need her to go. Far, far away. The last thing I need is for her to see what I have stashed in my locker. It's none of her business anymore.

I wish she would quit, and leave me to fry on my own. She could find a job anywhere. I'm trying not to resent Jordyn's CI, not to dwell on how easy she'd have it if she were mainstreamed, when my weeks at Finley have been so awful. People would love her immediately, since it takes no extra effort to accommodate her.

She gets both worlds. I'm totally and completely on my own.

"What's wrong?" she asks, reading my mind a little.

"Nothing," I sign one-handed, sipping the shake at the same time. *Nothing you'd understand anymore.*

"Hey"—Jordyn straddles the bench and sits next to me—"I need to ask you something." She looks anxious, her eyes darting around the room. I know what she's going to say. She's going to ask if I'll forgive her, even though she's done nothing to earn it. At least she'll be making a better apology than just texting "srry." Like I'm not even worth buying a vowel.

"You aren't still interested in Donovan, are you?" she asks, and immediately looks down at the dirty tiled floor. I tap her, forcing her to look at me.

"What?" I scowl.

"I mean, I know you used to like him. But that was forever ago, wasn't it?"

"Why?" This is what she wanted to ask me? What does Donovan have to do with us? With what happened between us and why she snitched? That's what I want her to talk about, not some stupid boy drama. Even if I did see him first.

"I was thinking about asking him out. That's all." She stands back up and zips her jacket. "I mean, I waited for you to make a move. You never did. I assumed you were over him." I can't say anything, my hands are frozen in midair. Jordyn keeps on going. "I think he's into me."

"Oh, do you?"

"Yeah, and he just broke up with that girl, the one with the green hair. You know, she works the morning shift?"

"Sure," I snipe.

"So, do you mind?" The way she asks cuts at me; it's so obvious she doesn't actually want to know what my answer is. Like she doesn't even notice or care that I'm not at Kingston with her anymore. She's swept it all under some dingy rug as if it never happened, but I can still see the lump. Her phone,

Jordyn's stupid phone, lights up and she starts texting. She waves it in the air and signs, "Later!"

"Yeah, later," I sign at her back, before flipping the bird at the closed door. And for the first time I'm glad I'm not at Kingston, glad I don't have to see her fake face every day. At least I can pretend I get paid to deal with her now. It wasn't enough that she got me kicked out of school, she had to take it a step further and go after Donovan.

Smoldering, I take the lid off the shake and chug the rest. The sweet coolness calms me, and I slowly begin to feel like myself again. I pop the lock open and slide it from the metal loop. I'm relieved she's finally gone. It's not that Jordyn would care if she knew what was in my locker, but I'm not going to take any more risks with her. Or anyone. I'd rather have everyone think that I put it all behind me. No more bragging, no more getting up. I'm not Julia.

I'm HERE.

I swing open my work locker. Inside are two backpacks: the one my mom checked and the one she didn't.

I leave most of it behind. I have no plans to go out writing tonight. I take out a Yakuza Yellow paint pen and my X-Acto knife kit. I'm pretty sure I can get away with my X-Acto, since Mee knows I use it to sharpen pencils. She doesn't know about the whole cutting-stencils bit. I'd like to keep it that way.

The lights flick off and on twice, my black bag hits the floor and one lone paint pen (Zombie Green) rolls across the tiles and collides with Donovan's boots.

We're frozen for a moment before I scramble to get my stuff back into my locker. By the time I look up at him, he's reading the fine print on the pen case. He shakes it, pops the lid off, and takes a deep whiff.

Donovan's lips are hard for me to read. I think it's equal parts his mumbling and my not being able to look at his mouth for too long without imagining, well, a lot of things. We don't talk much if Jordyn isn't around to interpret.

He caps the pen and holds it out. I can see that he's talking to me, but my heart is racing. *Get it together.* I hold both my hands up, more charades. Lately it feels like I'm some sort of caveman: *ME JULIA, YOU HOT BOY WORK DRIVE-THRU.* I bring my hands down through the air, nice and easy.

"Slow down," my hands say.

"Oh——-, sorry." He points to the marker with his other hand and gives me a thumbs-up. Then he points right at me.

"You," he mouths, "draw?" Donovan takes the marker and pretends to draw on his hand. At least he's trying. I place my hand out, palm down, and tilt it back and forth. I'm willing my lips to stay neutral but the corners are defying gravity.

"Cool." He hands me the pen and with a little wave goes off to start his shift.

There's only a million more things I wanted to say to him. Or, you know, have an actual conversation. But that's all I get with hearies. Hi. Bye. Thumbs up, thumbs down. Head nod. Friend, family, etc.

I talk with the Donovan that lives in my head the whole drive home.

"What're you doing here?" I ask coyly. "I thought you didn't have a shift today."

"I had to buy a new tire for Henry this week, so I had to pick up a night shift." His hands sign as deftly as a native speaker.

"Poor Henry. Give him my regards." Henry is the name I gave his car—not that he knows this.

"How's the new school?" he would ask.

"Rough going for now. I'm dying to get into this advanced art class, but it's full and the—"

"Advanced? I didn't know you were an artist."

"Oh. Well, you know, I'm okay. I guess."

"Can I see your stuff sometime?"

"Just drive under the overpass on Spring Road."

My eyes sting. That conversation would never happen, not even close. Who knows what he gets to talk with Jordyn about? A lot of things, I bet.

No tagging on a whim anymore, that's my new rule. But I need to feel like myself again; I need to be HERE. Screw it. *Thm! Thm! Thm!* There it is: that heart-pounding, finger-numbing adrenaline that surges through my head and radiates through the rest of my body. *Let's do this.*

I take Zombie Green out of my pocket. Normally I would use the yellow one, but I'm all about this pen now; it has a secret. This tag is a note, a journal entry. Today Donovan held this marker and asked me about art. I wasn't supposed to see him, and I did. He asked me about art, and I wanted to tell him everything, and since that's never happening, this will have to do.

I lace up my boots, pull on my hoodie, and hide the marker up my sleeve. I walk four blocks away from Lee, which should put enough distance between us, before I look around for the perfect spot.

I like to pretend I'm waiting for a bus when I'm scoping out a good place to write. I can't have it look like I'm wandering around without a purpose, but there's no bus stop here. The main street has more traffic than I would like, but tonight I want to feel the risk. There's a pizza place (closed), a drug store (closed), some mom-and-pop gift shop (closed), and the Dairy Barn (open). A car passes and a pedestrian-crossing sign is illuminated, all neon and yellow, in its headlights. *That's my spot.* The sign is directly across from Dairy Barn, but the drive-thru window faces the opposite street. It's a decent spot. I like pedestrian-crossing signs the best because of the little silhouetted people on them.

This pedestrian is Donovan, and he's saying my name. The art gods are on my side tonight; they know I need this and the roads are dead empty. I reach up and draw. When I'm tagging, the rest of the world blurs out. That can be really dangerous—another reason to keep it tight and work quickly.

My arm knows what to do before my brain even tells it to. I have this weird connection between my brain and my limbs, kind of like when hearing people say they talk without thinking sometimes. I move without thinking. I close my lines.

I've drawn a word bubble, and inside: HERE

I add a few of Donovan's perfect arm hairs for good measure. I cap it and scram. I don't stand around admiring, I don't take an Instagram. I write and run.

~(>_<~)

WHAM. THUNK.

That's me, getting hit in the head with a basketball, then hitting the floor. The ball is hurled at the back of my head, so I can't see it coming. Next they'll say I shouldn't be allowed to play. I feel like I'm back in middle school.

Let's get one thing straight: if I threw a basketball at the back of Kyle Fucking Stokers's head, he would hit the floor just as hard as I did. Deafness has nothing to do with it.

Gym is the one and only period I don't have my terp following me around, which makes it even worse. No one willing to play my version of charades with me, and there's no paper to write anything out on.

Casey is required to be in all my classes, including gym, but we struck a secret deal: I get some time without a chaperone, and she gets to pick up our lunches from somewhere less vile than the Finley cafeteria. Every time I have gym, I start to regret our arrangement, but then I see the processed meat slabs they serve at lunch and change my mind.

The floor is cold against my face. Nice floor, good floor. I must have really hit my head. I push against the nice, nice floor and roll onto my back. Ms. Ricker glares down at me, her whistle dangling over my face. She stands there, hands on her hips, doing nothing, while Yoga Pants comes running over to help. More gold stars for Yoga Pants. At least she looks more concerned for my well-being than Ricker, who is probably telling her to take me out back and shoot me.

I end up in the locker room, holding my thumping head in my hands. Yoga Pants takes a small bottle out of her gym bag and hands it to me: Extra Strength Tylenol.

"I——-headaches." She points to her head and squints.

"Thanks," I sign. I shake out two pills and gulp them down at the water fountain. Yoga Pants is talking to me, but the only word I manage to catch is *question*. She's skittish, pacing back and forth as she speaks. I reach out and place my hands on YP's rounded shoulders, and she finally stops talking. I point to my eyes, then to her mouth, and do my patented "slow down" gesture.

"Oh, oh! Sorry!" She actually uses the right sign for the word *sorry*. She looks at me straight on with her full, cherubic face. Her cheeks and heavy blond bangs remind me of that woman from Manet's painting *A Bar at the Folies-Bergère*. Pretentious, I know, but I can't help but see it. Paintings get stuck in my head in the same way I imagine songs get trapped in hearing people's ears.

"I ask you questions?" she says slowly, taking her time to mouth the words. I relent and nod my head. Right now I'll do anything so long as I don't have to go back into the gym.

"I'll make——like, yes-or-no ones. So you——-——nod for yes, shake for no, or whatever, okay?"

I just nod or whatever.

"Okay. So! Can you hear, like, anything?"

Shake.

"Whoa, nothing—all?"

Shake.

"You -----———-hearing-aid thingie?"

This is bigger than a yes-or-no question. I have hearing aids, but I hate them. They don't do anything but distract me, and I have awful tinnitus for hours after I take them out. I shake my head no.

"Was everyone deaf --———old school?"

I waggle my head, leaning toward yes. We had some hearing teachers, kids with cochlear implants, some people who were going deaf, some hard of hearing. A mixed bag. Not everyone who is deaf is profoundly so.

"Why did you leave?"

I look at my feet and pick at a cuticle. Should I tell her? Certainly not the whole story, maybe . . .

"Oh! Sorry"—with her fist on her chest she signs it again—"that's not a yes-or-no." I give her the benefit of the doubt. This is the first almost-conversation I've had at Finley with someone other than Casey, and it's all right. Even if her questions are the most basic hearie-meeting-a-Deafie-for-the-first-time ones. I point to myself.

"You . . . ," she repeats.

I kick my foot out, like I'm kicking a ball.

"Kick?"

I nod and throw my thumb back over my shoulder like an umpire making a call at first base. See, I know some things about sports.

"Um . . ."

I kick and thumb again.

"You got kicked out?" Her ice-blue eyes grow wide. She's excited to get a bit of gossip from me.

Nod. I point to myself again and she follows along. The bell in the girls' locker room is so loud I can feel it in my chest. I sign "later" to her and then point to my wrist for

31

extra clarity as the room fills up with girls rushing to get changed and get out.

Yoga Pants points to me, then to her head one last time. She doesn't talk when she signs, "You. Head." Thumbs up?

"Better," I sign back, swiping my chin. I assume she understands because the sign conveniently has a thumbs-up already built in.

"Good -----, Kyle. Great work." Ms. Ricker pats him on the back as he leaves the gym. *Great work?* Was she not in the same class I was just in? That's some serious selective memory. I've had it up to *here* with Kyle Fucking Stokers. I don't care how the game went, or how nice his eyebrows look. I'm standing here with my head throbbing from the ball he threw at me, and he gets an "attaboy"? I look over to Ricker and her eyes dart away from me.

"Hey!" I shout, not sure how loud I am.

"What?" Ms. Ricker scowls, confused. Good. I'm loud enough, then.

"He gets a pat on the back? What do I get?" The words scratch my throat as I yell them. The way he looks at me, like I'm a joke, takes my simmering blood up to a boil. He smirks, and one of his bros elbows him, chuckling.

"It was an accident." Kyle grins the fakest grin that ever graced his stupid face. "I'm sorry." He fakes the apology, so it's just genuine enough to be believable. I don't buy it for one second, but Ricker is obviously satisfied with his bullshit excuse. He almost winks at me on his way out of the gym.

"Don't walk away!" I shout, and chase after him. I grab at

him and my fingers brush the back of his jacket. Yoga Pants steps between us, grasping my hands. I thought I was angry before, but this? Holding my hands still, trying to shut me up? I wouldn't dream of putting a hand over a hearing person's mouth while they're talking. I try to wiggle away but she's holding tight, her eyebrows arched with that all-too-familiar expression: pity. I am on fire, I am HERE. *Don't pity me.*

"Let me go!" I scream and thrash until she releases my hands.

"Stop screaming!" Ricker finally butts in.

"You! Leave! Me——" I'm screaming and signing at the same time to everyone and no one in particular, until KFS leans in over Yoga Pants's shoulder.

"No——-understand you," he spits. "Get it? You're embarrassing yourself."

"Do————take——-to --- office?" Ricker separates us all. As far as I'm concerned, she's said the magic word. *Office.* God, what am I thinking? I can't handle getting kicked out of another school; I'm in enough shit as it is. Deep fucking breath. I back off.

"Okay——now get out——gym."

She hurries YP, Kyle, all of them out of the door. I lag behind in the gym entrance, my face flushed red and hot.

"Hey." Ms. Ricker hunches over slightly so our faces are on the same level. "I'm————wasn't—purpose. He said——-sorry. You're——-————yourself——favors." She doesn't look into my eyes as she talks to me, as if her ugly sneakers are more interesting than my face. "I————-it's great————you're——————-school——-——, but you're——-————try and fit in————-normal kids, okay? It'll make life————you."

She pats me on the back, a stiff hard thump that moves me through the doors of the gym.

I seethe, my boiling blood turning to acid. I think about sprinting to my car, to the road, to the underpass, anywhere but this spot. And as I think about it my legs take over for me and start running, down the hall, through the cafeteria, my eyes seeing red.

(" • _ • ")

Red flannel. Mini Mondrians woven all over his shirt. We collide and I almost fall to the ground for the second time today, but Mr. Katz steadies us both. He always seemed sort of gangly to me before, but he is able to catch me at full speed without toppling. A curl of black hair falls in his eyes as he studies my face for a moment. He exhales.

"Not a good day, huh?" he asks slowly enough for me to understand. No day here has been a good day. There have been days where I've slipped under the radar, but I wouldn't call those *good* days. He motions for me to follow him and walks down the hall without looking back.

I follow. I imagine what we must look like, him gliding along like a proud trumpeter swan, me waddling along in his wake like some pissed-off goose. When we get to Room 105, he unlocks the door and holds it open for me.

This is the room I've been dying to get into ever since I landed at Finley.

There are no desks, just long tables set up around the perimeter of the room. In the center stand two big lamps on tripods, their light framing a carefully draped table. On top sit some empty wooden buckets, a teakettle, four apples, and a pear. Still life isn't really my thing, but after a month of bad English papers and full-contact basketball, I could turn this into a masterpiece. The walls are covered in sketches, some of the still life on the table, others of previous still-life arrangements, and random drawings, too. Comic pages, a drawing of Mr. Katz, whatever. Brushes are drying in big paint-stained coffee cans. A record player sits precariously close to the slop sink. You would think he would be more careful with vintage electronics. The whole room has that sharpened-colored-pencil smell—nothing is clean but everything is perfect.

Mr. Katz doesn't have a desk but a podium with shelving underneath it. He fishes out a yellow legal pad and starts writing. When he's finished, he holds it out to me. He's written:

Stay and work awhile. It always helps me.

I take the yellow pad. The sunny paper shines up at me, saying this could be all right. I motion for his pen. It's one of those nice ones, the kind that feels heavy and expensive. I concentrate. Normally, I don't give a crap about my grammar. I got so sick of my old English teachers hammering away at us, saying we Deafies have to rise above the stereotypes, and I get it. I do. But I just don't care about commas and capitals and sentence structure. Just like I don't care about chemistry or U.S. history. I don't discriminate. I've never been one to set a good example anyway.

Still, I feel this pull, and a desire to impress him. I'm asking for a favor and I want to be understood. When it comes to art I don't like to be lazy. I take my time and write as clearly as I can.

May I join your class?

He scribbles a response, some excuse about it being the wrong time, and there's no room, and he wishes he could, and blah blah blah. I wave my hand to stop him and sign, "I know." He goes back to his first sentence and underlines the word *always*. Before I can respond Katz takes his pen, retrieves a tote bag from under the podium, and is at the door. He closes it behind him, gives a little wave through the window, and is gone.

He was right. How did he know that? That I would almost instantly feel better sitting here by myself, left alone to do what I do best. I decide to try my hand at the still life and take out my sketchbook. I don't feel right about helping myself to the supplies scattered around the room. I don't rack paint either, even though some writers would say that doesn't make me legit. I'm not a thief, I'm a vandal. That's why I work at Mickey D's: I buy my own supply.

I keep thinking about the pear: Why only one pear? Was there a sale on apples? Did he pick up the pear by mistake, thinking it was an apple? Or were the apples mistakes and he was sad to find out he got only one pear? I like this pear. I'll start there.

I begin sketching the base of the pear, where it's sitting. There is a nice little fold in the cloth underneath. Folds are tricky. I love the way they look, curvy and kind of sexy in a way. Which is probably why I'm not very good at drawing them yet. I'm better at hard lines and solid forms, like letters. My old art teacher told me I draw like a man. I've never forgiven him. I don't draw like anything, I draw like everything. I draw like me.

Folds in cloth and bumpy, organic-shaped pears make for a rocky start to my still-life adventure, but I'll be damned if I am going to walk out and give up this room. I'll get it right. The bucket in the background would have been no problem, all hard lines and wood. I fall in love with its little iron handle. Where do you even get a bucket like that anymore? I go back to shading in my pear. I'm not mad, not hungry, not anything. Just me in an empty room with my pencil and pad and pear.

I call it finished with about a minute to spare before either Mr. Katz comes back or the next class floods in, neither of which I want to be here for. I want to vanish like a ghost, savor this mood I'm in now. I carefully tear out my still life and pin it on the wall next to Mr. Katz's podium. It's from the last page in my sketchbook. His writing is in the corner, almost like a signature: *We'll see.*

We'll
see.

\\(° o° ;)

"**A**re you sure you don't want me to start coming to your gym class?" Casey follows me out to my car after school. Ricker must have told her what happened. I certainly didn't.

"I'm fine, don't worry about it."

"I do worry! Making some friends might help, too, you know." She's so genuine, I can't tell if she's making puppy-dog eyes or if it's just the magnification of her glasses.

"Don't have time for friends." And after Jordyn's dirty double-crossing sent me off to this place, don't want 'em, either. I'm meant to be an outsider. I highly doubt Banksy spends his weekends palling around with his BFF.

"Seriously, let me introduce you around to some of the kids in your lunch period. They aren't all bad."

I never thought I would be thankful to see Yoga Pants walking toward me, but here I am. I wave at her and smile. She barely nods and keeps walking. Shit, was I that harsh in gym? I wave at her again with a bit more enthusiasm. She heads over to us.

"This is my friend," I sign to Casey.

"Really. You're friends?" Casey asks YP without signing. YP looks over to me, her eyebrows screwed up and confused. I smile and nod, pleading with my eyes.

"Sure, why not." YP signs the word for *friend*.

40

I sign and Casey jumps at the chance to interpret for a peer: "Julia wants to know if you would like to go to Dairy Barn with her."

"Oh, Julia! That's your name?" YP blurts. *Come on now, play it cool, we're "friends," remember?*

"This is YP," I sign to Casey, introducing her.

"YP? What?" Casey signs with that puzzled look of hers.

"It's her name sign." Another lie, but whatever, it's a fine name sign.

"You gave her a name sign?" To YP: "She gave you a name sign?" *Crap.* Casey has been bugging me for one since I met her. I've kind of resisted on principle.

"What's a name sign?" YP asks us both.

"It's a sign for your name," Casey explains. "So you don't have to fingerspell your name every time you say it. You can't make up your own, you have to be given one by a Deaf person." Casey can't help but teach her.

"How do you sign yours?" YP asks Casey. I'm tapping my feet, trying to ride out the good feelings from drawing earlier. This is about to be a buzzkill.

"I don't have one yet." Casey looks so disappointed, and I feel the slightest pang of guilt. Look, I'm not going to just give a name sign to everyone who asks, as if it would make them some sort of official member of the Deaf Club. I wave to get YP's attention.

"My name sign is—" I'm signing to her, but I can see Casey translating.

I show her how to make the hand shape for my name. Mee gave it to me when I was little, and sadly it stuck. It goes along with her whole "my girls are precious jewels" thing.

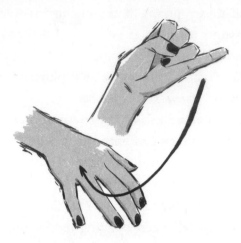

"Let's go!" I point to the road, changing topics.

"Can we walk?" YP makes her fingers into little legs and wiggles them. "It's so nice out."

"Sure." I nod yes and head far away from Casey.

It's true, the weather is golden. It's one of those fall days where you start out wearing a coat but forget it on a bench or something because why would you have brought a coat, look how nice it is outside! We cross the street and head toward Dairy Barn.

We don't have a Dairy Barn in my neighborhood in Queens Village. I've never even gone to one before. Greenlawn has at least three of them. At home I'd just go to a bodega, but there aren't too many of those out here in the suburbs. I'm not exactly sure what the appeal of Dairy Barn is, but it seems like everyone goes and gets either chocolate milk or iced tea. I didn't even think about it when I asked YP. It's ingrained into the Finley subconscious: Want to hang out after school? Go to Dairy Barn, get iced teas.

"How's your head?" She points to the back of mine.

"Fine," I sign, mouthing the word for her. YP immediately copies me. This is going to be another long-ass beginner conversation. I take out my cell phone and mime for her number. I plug it into my contacts and text her.

JULIA: Hey. Easier to chat if we text.

YP: Cool!

JULIA: Thanks for covering the "friend" thing.

YP: What do you mean?

JULIA: Just thanks for sayin that.

YP: Yeah sure.

Both of us look at our screens, walking, neither of us really knowing what to say. She was nice enough in the locker room, but I'm not really sure we have all that much in common.

JULIA: Your aspirin really saved my head.

YP: Np - that sucked.

JULIA: Kyle makes me (ಠ ∩ಠ)

YP: Ha. Yea.

She looks up from her phone. Her shoulders droop as she exhales. What now? Something I said?

JULIA: You OK?

YP: Hes my ex.

I knew that Yoga Pants wasn't exactly the kind of girl who would run with outcasts like me. She could easily have been one of those thicker cheerleaders who holds the feather-weights up in the air. She could be on the softball team, or not even play a sport, she's pretty enough to score a cute guy and be popular by association. However all that shit works.

But dating KFS? I was just starting to think she had more sense than that. He doesn't even try to hide his doucheness. Doesn't have to, I guess. It's a letdown, YP going for someone like that. The confession is a bummer, but she doesn't owe me anything.

JULIA: His loss.

YP: I guess.

JULIA: I know.

She sighs and signs to me, pulling her hands far apart and then bringing them together like a book.

"Long story."

"OK," I sign. Probably best to drop it.

"Maybe I———learn——alphabet. ————-help, right?" she asks.

JULIA: U don't have to.

YP: Why not?

JULIA: ¯_(°_°)_/¯ Dunno. seems like a lot of
work or whatever.

Every time someone offers to learn ASL, they bail. They
realize that it's actually a whole language and give up when it
gets hard. Suddenly I'm not so fascinating anymore and they
move on to some other obsession. It makes me miss Jordyn,
and Kingston for that matter. Just being able to talk without
having to figure out some workaround. Jordyn and I would
sit up and talk until my fingers hurt.

Dairy Barn is a funny place. It really looks like a little barn,
painted red with a fake silo. There's nowhere to sit inside except for one stool for whoever's working there. The whole
store is like a supermarket dairy aisle, except as a drive-thru.
Donovan's nightmare, I bet. But they don't have an intercom:
you pull up, tell the attendant what you want, and pay all in
one go. I type out on my cell:

TWO LARGE ICED TEAS

We walk up to the window and I hold up my phone and debit
card. The man working at the window chuckles.

"Cat got your tongue?" he asks. It always baffles me when
people think I'm just typing things out to be different. Or
lazy. My new favorite is when they say it's my generation.
Damn millennials, never off their stupid phones! No, you able-
ist jerkwad. This is how I'm going to communicate with you.

I point to my ear and mouth the word *deaf*. This usually is enough to get my point across. His nose turns red, his eyes glance back and forth between me and my phone. He realizes he screwed up.

"Oh, sorry, sweetheart, ——-no idea."

I lift my arms as if to say, *Oh, well!* YP looks mortified. I just wish he hadn't called me sweetheart.

"Here, it's on me," he says as he nervously hands us each a cup. Normally, I would complain and tell him not to treat me differently than any other customer, but hey, free drinks.

YP: Whoa, he was pretty embarrassed huh?

JULIA: Oh well! TB.

YP: ??

JULIA: Too bad

She gives me a funny look, but obliges anyway, and we "clink" Styrofoam cups. One sip of the famous iced tea and my mind explodes. Bye-bye, Red Bull—this stuff is like crack. It's insanely, sickly sweet, but you can still taste the lemon and tea flavors underneath. Unlike the stuff that comes from the school vending machine, this doesn't have a bit of sour aftertaste; it doesn't coat your tongue in that syrupy, chemical way. It's amazing. I'm so busy swooning over bliss-in-a-cup that I almost miss it: my tag on the crossing sign. My little love note to Donovan in Zombie Green.

Someone wrote over it.

It hasn't been buffed off or anything—someone's calling me out. They're dissing me.

My heart skydives into my stomach. So soon? I haven't seen any good graff around here, and already someone's trying to throw down? YP looks up at the sign with me and points.

"Huh,———-kind—cool, no?" I stop reading her lips. What is she even talking about? Cool? More like insulting. I'm not HERE? Where, then? Why not? Who are you to tell me what and where and who?

"Um . . . come on." She pulls me away from the sign and I let her, not wanting YP to catch on to me. Maybe it was some toy acting stupid. I'm jumping to conclusions. That's all it is. Some punk kid trying to step to my game, and making a fool out of themselves, frankly, because they turned my writing into a drippy mess.

As we head back to the school, I focus on the weather and the walk and the iced tea, concentrating on sipping and not chatting. It feels good to give my hands and mind a rest. They make reading lips look so easy on TV: every deaf character has absolutely perfect lip-reading superpowers. But in reality it's inaccurate, and *exhausting*. Not all of us are good at it. People don't get that.

"This is *your* car?" YP dances over to Lee and puts her hands on the trunk. "It's amazing! I was————-whose it was. I————might be Mr. Katz's.——-into this———— thing."

"Really?" I sign.

"Totally, it's so beautiful!" I guess she's talking loudly because two girls start watching us from across the parking lot.

"——-—-bad I don't have a car, I would—" One of the girls glares and snickers. They huddle closer, talking.

47

"Oh—" YP stops herself midsentence. "I should --- -----.
See you in history." I place my hand on her shoulder as she's
about to go and pull out my phone.

JULIA: Don't worry . . . I'm used to it.

YP: Theyre not laughing at *you*

(π_π)

All I can think about during dinner is what happened to my tag and what I should do about it. The takeout from Rajdhani's isn't much of a distraction. If some toy wants to come along and wreck my work, I'm just going to have to make it more challenging. It was my first tag in town and the paint was barely dry before it got done up. My chicken makhani is cold by the time I take another bite.

"I got a call this afternoon." Mee snaps me out of my fog.

"You haven't been . . . ?" Ma looks shocked.

"No!" I sign with extra emphasis. Not anywhere the school would know about, anyway.

"No, no, this isn't about that." Mee looks over at Ma, then back at me. "What happened at gym class?" she asks, probably knowing full well what happened. Is this why she cracked and got us Indian again this week? She knows it's my comfort food, so she's trying to soften the blow of her planned confrontation? I guess the school finally figured out how to make a Video Relay Service call. I was kind of hoping they wouldn't, so my hearing teachers and Deaf parents would never, *ever* communicate. I wonder who interpreted that call between an angry hearing teacher and a pair of Deaf parents. Did the terp take my side or theirs? Probably neither.

"Just some dude, mainstream-garbage stuff." I break eye contact and chew on a lukewarm slice of naan.

"Is that *all*?" Mee leans in, trying to squeeze info out of me like Mr. Howard. Do all adults use this tactic? They should just come out with what they know and let you apologize. Don't hand me a shovel and make me dig the grave deeper.

"I was upset, he was rude. They called you for that? I'm fine now. It's over."

"Casey says you yelled at a teacher," Mee continues. She's obviously very concerned. Her brown eyes droop and she brushes my hair off of my shoulder.

Ma places the clear plastic lid on top of her container of biryani, signaling she's ready for battle. "You did what?!" Ma signs. "You couldn't be peaceful and respectful, after everything that's happened?" Ma, a teacher herself, will always side with one. This is the worst thing for her to find out right now and it shows. Her hands, so similar to mine, sign with purpose. Every movement is sharp and swift. She chews on her bottom lip when she's especially angry. Like now.

"Ma, you don't understand!" Casey wasn't even there, and now she's calling my parents? This is way, *way* out of bounds. Usually my mothers would see that, and they'd put an overstepping interpreter in her place. But of course, just as I suspected, they're using Casey as an extra set of watchful eyes on their little vandal. No wonder they didn't go through the system to find an interpreter. They have Casey in their pocket. Why should they trust me? I'm only their daughter.

"I do! I do understand," Ma says. "You knew going to a mainstream school would be difficult, but you brought this experience on yourself. You don't get to act out when things don't go your way."

"That's not what happened!"

"What am I going to do with you? We work so hard to—"

50

"Cara." Thankfully, Mee cuts her off. I've heard this speech way too many times since leaving Kingston. "Even though she's made a mistake, that doesn't mean she can't feel upset."

"There is no excuse for yelling at a teacher!"

I stand up, ready to fight. Why does it feel like I'm always fighting lately? But Ma's eyes are wide and alert; this isn't one of those nights where she's had a few glasses of wine and I can make a dent in her argument. Ma is on an unshakable streak, standing up for teachers everywhere. She won't hear me or Mee. Debating her will only make things worse. Once again, I'm forced to surrender.

"You're right. Won't happen again." I shove my chair against the table and head for the basement.

How am I supposed to unpack this day? Sweating, I yank my hoodie over my head and hurl it across the room. I start turning on my lamps one by one. I hate the harsh overhead fluorescent lighting we have in the basement. It was never meant to be a workspace, only storage. It's not one of those nice finished, hang-out-with-your-girlfriends, have-a-sleepover-type basements. Even so, I keep begging my parents to let me turn it into my bedroom. I spend 90 percent of my home life down here anyway.

I collected the lamps from some thrift shops. One is this old cracked faux-Tiffany glass thing; another is a bunch of illuminated plastic balloons, a little clown holding the strings. And a huge purple lava lamp, the catch of a century that Jordyn and I found in someone's trash. I remember having to carry it for thirty blocks because Jordyn didn't feel like waiting for the LIRR. She gabbed and gabbed the whole way home, but I can't for the life of me remember what about. I do know that I couldn't really respond with more than a nod, because this beast of a lamp is heavy as shit. I don't turn that one on. I don't know if I ever will again.

I sink down into my work chair. Mee bought it for me ages ago. It's my command center. I do all my work from here.

She said she doesn't care if I get paint or ink all over it, that it was mine to make use of. When I got expelled, I only felt guilty about one thing: letting her down. Mee's never told me not to draw or pursue art. Even when she doesn't understand my work, she tells me she loves it. When she found out what I did, though, a ten-foot-tall slab of concrete went up between us, and I dare not paint on it. Before, I kind of thought she might even like the fact that I was going public, but yeah, not so much. The boots were the one sign that forgiveness is possible.

I click on the last lamp that hangs over where I sit. One of those round crinkly paper lanterns, big and yellow, it shines over me like the sun. It's the only place I actually appreciate a spotlight, where I don't wish some fog would roll in and envelop me in obscurity.

I take out my X-Actos and a charcoal pencil from my lucky mug with all the strawberries on it and get to sharpening. I like really hard pencils and charcoals—5H is primo. I'll settle for HB if I have to, but anything softer than that, and I can only draw for sixty seconds before I'm sharpening again. Soft pencils just don't last, and when you buy your own supply, you need that shit to get you through more than one drawing.

As I hack away at the pencil, every crappy thing that has happened to me the past few weeks replays in my head. Over and over.

Getting expelled.

Shunk.

Getting expelled over art that no one even remembers.

Shunk.

Being assigned to the world's most annoying terp.

Shunk.

Having to need a terp at all, at a stupid mainstream school.

Shunk.

A school where people think I'm an idiot.

Shunk.

Where I can barely talk to anyone at all.

And when I do they can't understand me.

And give me shit for it.

And throw things at me.

And get away with it.

And I get the blame.

Shunk.

Shunk.

Shunk.

Shunk.

Shunk.

SHIT.

Blood flows from my left index finger. I grab my hand tightly, double over in pain, and cry out. I slide off of my chair onto the floor, pencil shavings clinging to my black leggings. Sucking air in through my teeth, I let the pressure off my finger and assess the damage: it's still attached but it's dripping red. Holy shit, it felt like I cut the damn thing off. I stick my finger in my mouth and it fills with that weird metallic taste. Taking deep breaths through my nostrils, I try to calm myself down. I'm shaking. Blood and I don't really get along.

When my finger quits throbbing against my tongue, I take it out for a closer inspection. So much blood for such a minor cut. I might have a tiny scar, but it's really not too bad. In the open air it starts to sting and pulse again. I wrap the finger up as tight as I can in the hem of my shirt, willing the pain to go away. I thought I could handle it. I'm supposed to not care.

Tears find their way into the corners of my eyes but I refuse to let them fall. I bury my face in the cushion of my beautiful armchair, my command center, and scream. Over and over, my throat vibrating and crackling with fire. Nobody comes to see what's wrong. Nobody can hear me.

`\(o _° )/`

It's nine billion degrees standing over the fryer this morning. The Sunday morning shift might be my very favorite, though. I can tell the difference between french-fry smell and hash-brown smell, and I prefer the latter. It's a bit after eight and the actual work hasn't picked up speed yet, but the fryers are running full blast.

I'm going to Urban Café after my shift to make a paint order. I've had enough drama; it's time to get to work. I'm debating between hitting up that spot near the Little League field and doing a big pen piece in one of the bathroom stalls in the Greenlawn Diner. I don't feel ready for the overpass yet. I'll probably go with the field, more public, more—

There's a little pinch on my waist and I snap back to reality. Donovan flashes me a smile and points to my blinking timer. Whoops. I pull the browns from the oil and hook the baskets up so they can drip for a second.

"What's up?" he signs.

"Nice signs." I shake my hand, impressed.

"Jordyn taught me." Unfortunately, I read his perfect lips. *Thanks, Jordyn.*

"More, please," I sign, my fingertips touching.

"Kiss you? Damn, girl." He plants a big one on my cheek and heads past me to his station. Suddenly it's fifteen billion degrees and I am but a puddle on the floor, no bones, just thoughts and feelings. He looks back over his shoulder at me and chuckles. I assume it's because the expression on my face must look something like a cross between HOLY FREAKING UNICORNS RIDING ON MAGICAL GLITTERING RAINBOWS and DEAD. And to put the cherry on top of my melted Mickey D's sundae of feelings, he actually winks at me. The bastard.

This is the sign for *more:*

This is the sign for *kissing:*

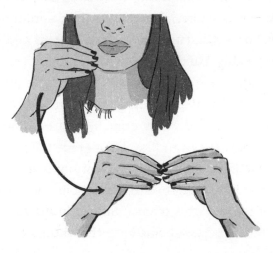

I can see why he got confused—the signs have the same hand shapes and all—but it's not really a hard one to mess up in terms of context. *What's up? Kiss me!* Doesn't that sound like a bit of a leap? Jesus. I'm a brave person, but Jesus.

Speaking of Him, church must have just let out, because the lines start to grow, drive-thru gets hectic, and orders start flying up on the screen. *Fry! Fry! Fry!* It's pretty cute when parents bring their kids after church, all pouty in their patent-leather shoes and polo shirts, exhausted moms and dads bribing them to behave during Mass so afterwards the kids can pray in their molded plastic pews to the gods of cheap toys and Happy Meals and french fries, amen.

I fill up a bunch of small fry bags, knowing how many Happy Meals are about to get ordered, and it hits me—of course he knows the sign for *kissing*. Why would Jordyn teach him anything else? The thought of them making out leaves a bad taste in my mouth. I thank God she isn't working today.

Something changes. Donovan raises his shoulders, his arms tense up. He starts pacing in what little space the windowed area allows. Checking the monitor, shuffling around the take-out bags. Oh, crap. Drive-thru drama.

The first thing I like to do when I notice things going downhill is put a big batch of fries down. The gush of hot steam, millions of bubbles rushing to the surface, means business. I know if an order has gone wrong or if someone is acting hellacious, Donovan likes to upgrade their fries, so it's best to overprepare at this point. Twenty billion degrees.

The next car pulls up to the window. It's a minivan with some sort of Little League team crammed in the back like sardines. The owner is pissed. She keeps checking her watch and screaming into the backseat. She also has one of those Blue-tooth receivers wedged in her ear. How do hearies listen to so many things at once? It must be maddening. She peeks above her oversized sunglasses and snaps at Donovan. He's trying to calm her down. He hasn't even lost his temper yet when the manager, Arnold, comes and taps me on my shoulder.

"Bring——bagsover—-mepleasewouldja?" He hands me five stuffed paper bags and dashes back to the office, talking into his own headset. He talks way too damn fast. I pull the fries out of the oil with one hand and make my way to the window. I place the bags between Donovan and Mrs. Soccer-hockey-tee-ball Mom.

"Excuse me! No!" She must be yelling. She jerks away from the window.

"I don't want Muslim hands touching my food! Or the children's." She turns and wraps her arms around the boy in the passenger seat, who looks as confused as I do. Some things I wish I didn't lip-read. Just because I'm brown doesn't mean I'm Muslim. Not that it should even matter. Take your hate to Chik-fil-A. My only god is Banksy. I hold my hands up and back away. Donovan offers his fry-upgrade tranquilizer and it seems to work. We head over to my station. Out of sight, he pretends to refill the bags. He motions for me to add the extra fries.

I reach for one of the colder bags—as if she deserves any-thing for free; why should she get the good stuff?—Donovan holds the take-out bag open, and I drop the fries in, but the Band-Aid from my X-Acto slash slides in with them. Sweat and the heat, I guess. We both look up at each other, stunned.

"Screw her," he says, and takes the bag to the window.

I can't believe we served that lady a no. 4 with a side of

scabs. I guess she was too rushed to notice, because she never came back. I try to forget her, and what she said. I'm thankful I don't have to hear her voice ringing in my head. All those kids, though. I feel bad for them, I wish they didn't have to hear that shit. No one should.

After my shift I get both backpacks from my locker; the black bag needs a resupply. This means it will spend a night under the driver's seat and some time hanging in my school locker. It'll be a tricky week.

Donovan comes into the locker room, already halfway through unbuttoning his shirt. *Don't look. Don't look.* He straddles the bench next to my locker, practically defining the word *swag*. Pretending to ignore him, I zip up my hoodie. He waves up at me. Okay, fine, you have my attention.

"Sorry———-that woman." He points over his shoulder.

"It's nothing." I wave the thought out of the air. "She was psycho." He understands because I use the classic pointer finger making circles near my temple motion.

"Ha-ha! Yeah," he laughs. I win. "So, you and Jordyn are tight, right?"

"Yeah . . ." Moment killed. Jordyn finds a way to ruin everything.

"I———take her————-cool, you know, like a date?" Can he tell how hard I'm scowling on the inside? I act like I don't know what he's asking. I wish I didn't.

"Oh, sorry." He looks at the ground. He's mad that I can't understand him. At least he doesn't realize I'm faking it. There's just no way I'm helping set them up.

I grab my black bag, fling it over my shoulder, and bang my locker shut. I wave on my way out, but he stops me. He points to my bag, and I feel like I have to get my eyes checked.

He can't possibly be gesturing the words *spray paint*. There's no way.

"What?" I keep pretending that I don't understand. He points to my bag, and once again crooks his index finger and moves it back and forth in front of me, spraying invisible paint in the air.

"No." I lift my shoulders, shake my head. *Who, me?* Of course not. Donovan tilts his head and looks at me and my black bag with more skepticism than Casey did when I told her I had friends.

"But—" He points out all the paint on my hoodie. Grabbing at the cuffs, he runs his thumbs along the stained ribbing. I yank my hands away, as much as it pains me to. Crap, I've got to get rid of it.

"See you later!" I sign with a smile, and hurry past him. I never thought I'd be running from Donovan, but even he can't know about this.

(-_-)>c[_][_P<(-_-)

Black bag stashed underneath the passenger seat, I pull into Urban Café's parking lot. It's closer to school, far from my home base. They love me in Urban Café. There, I'm this polite little deaf girl who comes in for treats and to write her school papers. In my head I call myself Melissa, bat my eyelashes, and wear my old hearing aids (turned off) for extra it's-rude-to-stare points.

It's not a cozy place. The lights are too bright and the floor is white tile. There isn't a little section with couches or armchairs, no fake library on the wall. All they have is tables, chrome chairs, and the counter. I imagine it was a frozen-yogurt place that folded, and the new owners couldn't be bothered to change the vibe. Anyway, the hot chocolate comes with homemade marshmallows, and that's what keeps me coming back.

I take my drink to my seat and fire up my laptop. I check the Stencil Bomb forums to see if someone was foolish enough to post a picture of their lame diss on my tag. There's a section for Long Island, but I get bored after combing through page after page of weak tags and lazy work. Amateurs posting hurried, dripping hate-paints. I can't stand them.

I log in. I have to post something. This is so unacceptable.

H3R3: This shit gives us bad names. Why you think everyone want to lock up writers and artists? Because of people like you. What you adding to the world by doing this?? Nothing. Keep your hate out of our game. ELEVATE. Get on our level, or get out.

I log into my Hush*mail* account and there's nothing new. This is the sort of thing you have to do to avoid getting busted by someone worse than your principal. Free Wi-Fi, incognito mode, an encrypted email address to make paint orders from, and a place—

Crap. I used to ship paint to the mailroom at Kingston. There was this work-study college guy that stuffed envelopes who I made friends with. Okay, I made out with him. A few times. Maybe more than a few times. He would set aside my boxes, and I would come grab them at the end of the day when the halls were chaotic. It was Jordyn's idea. She would hang out in the hall and get a kick out of my attempts to flirt. Once, after I picked up an abnormally large order, she told me I looked like a horrible kisser.

I think he knew what was in them, but he never said anything about it. So maybe I'm not such a bad kisser after all. Or he really liked me. Maybe both. It doesn't matter, because I can't show my face *there* anymore.

I have to order paint online because I'd get carded in person. Before the whole mailroom scheme, I would just send it to my house. My moms wouldn't even think to ask what I was ordering, and if they did, I'd show them. "Working on a project," I'd say, and they wouldn't even question it.

I decided it was a bad idea to keep sending it to my house

when I read on one of the forums that a kid got pinched that way. I was lucky that Mail Boy turned out to be pretty cute.

Now what the hell am I gonna do? I can't mail paint to McDonald's. I'm not going to start racking; one charge on my rap sheet is enough, thank you very much. I consider if I'm old enough to open a P.O. box.

This is why my grades are tanking. After all the effort I put into my career, there isn't much energy left over for all this reproductive-system-of-a-frog junk. Who even needs to know about that?

What a bust. I have only three cans left and the paint levels are dangerously low.

YP: I'm so bored.

JULIA: Whats up?

YP: Nothing to do on sundays not even good TV

JULIA: Im @ Urban Cafe

YP: Be there in 10

I don't know why I invited her. It just happened.

There's a tap on my shoulder and YP practically skips into the seat next to me. Her nose is pink from the cold, and it only adds to the cheeriness of her face. She grins and looks at her watch.

"Eight minutes --- fifty———-seconds! A—-record!"

"You ran here?" I can see she's panting a bit.

"Yep! Me, go, O R D E R," she signs, fingerspelling, and bounces off to the counter. This can't be her first coffee of the day. I take a minute to log out of everything, erase my history, clear my cache, and close my laptop.

Yoga Pants—today's pair are a dark shade of blue—heads back to our table and carefully puts her mug down. I was expecting her to get some sort of soy-caramel-extra-whip-extra-foam-type drink but no, it's plain black coffee. Before she starts fumbling through her signs again, I wave my phone, indicating we should text.

"Oh! Totally." She pulls out her cell and all her bubbles burst at once. Staring at the screen, unblinking, her eyes start to glaze over before little pools of tears well up in the corners.

"You OK?" I fingerspell for her.

"Yeah, 'scuse me for a sec." She puts her phone facedown on the table and heads to the bathroom.

What the hell happened? Her phone taunts me from her side of the table. I can't imagine anything that would dull her sparkle that fast, unless they were gonna close down Claire's, or Taylor Swift decided to quit music, or someone was kidnapped and texting for ransom, or someone, you know, died. Yikes. I reach for the phone. *No, no, I can't. I'm no snoop, I'm not going to just—*

KATIE: Your not bad at cheer.
    just gross in the uniform now.
    No 1 wants 2 see that.

I try to unlock her phone to get to the rest of the thread, but I don't know her passcode. It's not 1234. That one text says enough, though. I know what it's like to get a text like that. I get them in real time, real life, every day at Finley. I want to get that bitch's number and text back, tell her to fuck off, shove it, and die in a fire for insulting someone like that. But I don't. YP shuts the bathroom door, and I slip her phone more or less back where it was.

"Sorry." YP rubs her fist on her chest. I flip her phone faceup and she looks deep into her mug.

"D E L E T E," I spell, and point to the phone. She looks up at me, angry. She could rightfully blow her top over my snooping, but she doesn't. She opens her newly glossed lips to say something, but reconsiders and shakes her head. I finger-spell again, "D E L E T E."

"Why? Damage—————-done." She pushes the phone away from her. I pull out mine and start typing. Her phone vibrates on the table.

JULIA: Words are only words.

JULIA: People speak words about me all the time.
You kno what??

JULIA: I can't hear them so I let them say whatever.

JULIA: The words dont make you.
YOU make you.

She rolls her eyes, but I notice the slightest upturn in the corner of her lips. She points at my laptop, changing the subject.

YP: What were you working on?

JULIA: Dumb class project

YP: Mr. Katzs artist report?

JULIA: No! I wish. not in his class.

YP: Why not!!?!? Youre so good!

JULIA: How do you know?

YP: Your car!

JULIA: Oh! No room in his class for me

YP: Thats super unfair.

JULIA: RIGHT? Its the only class I really wanna take

YP: jerks. they could like totally pull up an extra dang chair.

JULIA: Why cant i get one good part to my day, you know?

JULIA: Makes me crazy!
(⊙_◎)

YP: Not your fault you came to school late.

JULIA: Well . . .

Her hands cover her mouth, eyes wide. I assume she's apologizing but I can't tell. You can't read lips when they're hidden. I pull her hands away from her face.

"Sorry!" she signs. "I————-forgot———-E X P E L L E D."

"Doesn't matter," I sign. It's cute how flustered she is, like I'm embarrassed about getting expelled. I'm not, but I'm sure she would be mortified if it happened to her.

I bet we look so perfectly normal, two cute girls drinking their hot beverages, texting away, not even looking at each other. We could be anyone, not some deaf chick and the girl who took pity on her. Just BFFs.

But we aren't, and I can't go spilling the beans to anyone. Yes, everyone at Kingston knew why I got kicked out, and no one was surprised. Jordyn wasn't the only person who knew about my penchant for spray paint, but she was the only person who snitched. Everyone knew I was the girl with the spray paint. The only clue about that part of my life now is Lee, and I guess my hoodie, but I'm taking care of that tonight.

JULIA: Feel better?

I text her as we start bussing our table. She's bouncing again.

YP: Little bit. Gonna jog back, thatll help

JULIA: I can drive.

YP: No way . . . I need it.

She pulls her sweater down around her hips. I don't get it, the nasty text, the jogging. YP isn't skinny, but she's not gross or ugly or whatever that text said. She's downright pretty. Shiny hair, blue eyes . . . So she's not skinny. So what?

JULIA: nah, youre a beauty.
(❀°‿°)

YP: Nothing big is beautiful

(^) /占~~~~~

After YP jogs off, I drive around for a while in my paint-stained hoodie. One last night together, gotta make it count.

I considered tagging another street sign, drawing a hoodie on Mr. Silhouette in tribute. It seems too small now. Too small, and too easy for someone to retaliate. I head over to the park where the Little Leaguers must play in the spring.

I've been eyeing the backs of the scoreboards for a month. There's one in particular that's low to the ground, so I wouldn't need to climb up anything. Definitely not a heaven piece, but I don't feel the need to put my life on the line. Not yet anyway. The field is empty at dusk, and it helps that it's starting to get really cold outside. I probably won't have to worry about some kid walking up on me.

Dusk isn't the prime hour for writing. The farther away I park, the longer it will take me to get back to the field. By then it will be darker. I take my ID out of my wallet and put it in my front pocket, leaving my phone and the wallet in the glove compartment. My car key and my house key go under the inserts in my boots. I know how noisy keys can be. *[Keys jingling]* is in, like, every closed-captioned movie ever.

My black bag is not your standard L.L. Bean or whatever kind of backpack. It *looks* like one, nothing fancy, just a plain black backpack. But on the inside, I sewed in a false back with a zipper you can only access once it's open, and even then, it's hard to spot.

On the *real* inside there are holsters for six loaded cannons. Though after what happened at Kingston, I never carry more than three cans on me. The elastic holsters ensure the cans don't jostle around if I have to run. It's hard enough running with a backpack, let alone one with a bunch of junk bouncing around inside.

I have a speckled notebook in the front compartment, and a few school flyers. Nothing heavy. That's all I bring. I've debated wearing my old hearing aids so I could better sense someone approaching, but I refuse. I get through every day without them; I'm not going to "cheat" and put them on when it's convenient.

The sky darkens and the chill in the air intensifies. I'm not freezing, but I'm hardly comfortable. I wish I had a heavier coat instead of just the hoodie, but the cold air will force me to work quickly. Get in, get out, get back to my nice warm Lee.

What am I gonna say? What goes into this throwie? My last tag was for Donovan; what should this one remind me of? I never throw up a meaningless piece. It's always attached to a memory, something I'll recall every time I see it. It isn't about seeing my art on a wall. It's about putting a feeling out into the world. It's communication, a release.

Maybe I'll paint my new tag, my new name, my new place in this hood. All done up nice and clean and big. Big. I can't stop thinking about YP. About big beautiful things.

What did she mean, "nothing big is beautiful"? I pull the cords in my hood taut. What a dumb thing to say. People will always be jerks. Always. Doesn't mean mountains aren't beautiful. Or redwood trees, or oceans, or—

I've made it up to the waist-high chain-link fence in the outfield and suddenly I'm not so cold. The kindling catches; the fire's coming.

I thought the back of the scoreboard would be a slam, too public, standing right in the middle of the field. But it casts a large shadow in my direction, and shadows are a lifesaver. Stepping into its dusky protection, I disappear. I slide my bag around to my chest and open the inner compartment. The new latex gloves don't keep my fingers warm, but I'll be sweating in no time. I grab the first can. Bruised Gray, a faded purple color. It looks handsome against the dark green of the scoreboard.

I start outlining the basic shape first. My arm works diligently. It must have had these plans for a while, filed away somewhere deep, because the shape almost draws itself.

I move as quickly as I can. I've practiced these techniques so many times, they're second nature. As soon as I finish the outline I start filling it in with the same color. It's important to be fast, but how you fill in shapes distinguishes the toys from the real writers.

It's getting even darker out, so I don't hesitate moving on to the next step. My heart races along with the passing minutes; beads of moisture form and drip down my spine. I holster the gray back in my bag. Next up: Cyanide Blue outlines. Normally, the outline stage moves the quickest for me. It's pretty much a repeat of step one, except this time I add more detail. This isn't just letters, though; it needs more volume, texture. I want to make this big thing beautiful.

Capped and holstered, I'm ready for the last step. I unsheathe Siamese Sesame from the bag and get to it. I wish

I had another color for this bit. Some bright white would really make it stand out, but the dusty beige will have to work. It's all I have. I need a really tight stream of paint to do the final details. I dig through my bag in the dark, trying to find my stencil cap. My fingers wrap around the little piece of plastic when the lights around the perimeter of the field flicker on.

I slam my body into the scoreboard, grateful only for the longer shadow it's casting. *Shit shit shit*. I was so close to finishing. A car or two passes. I go from flames to frozen stiff. I should be running to my car. I should be driving home. *Legs! Why aren't you running?!*

No one's coming. I peer around the board onto the diamond: empty. Maybe the lights are on a timer, I reason. *Finish it, finish it. You're so close.*

I take in a deep breath and hold it. It's up to my lungs how much time I have left. It's my own timer system. I snap the stencil cap in place. Final touches demand the finest lines. My arm flies across the board. A tan mist trails behind my hand. Each puff adds a detail, a little touch that brings the whole thing to life.

My lungs are shredding. Tension rips through my chest. I run my gloved finger through the wet paint on the last little beige circle. My work looks right back at me. It's the biggest, most beautiful piece I've ever done. My gift to Greenlawn. You're welcome, Universe.

I can't hold it anymore. I exhale, coughing and dizzy. The paint goes back into my bag. I zip the inside zipper and then the outer one. I'm an action hero, walking away from an explosion. I'm so awesome I don't even look back.

I ditch the used gloves in a garbage can and walk a few more blocks over to the Walgreens parking lot. They have these big clothing donation bins there. All I'm wearing underneath the hoodie is my ratty old Wonder Woman T-shirt. I didn't think about the weather. What a day to go braless. Doesn't matter; I'll freeze for a few more blocks. I finished my piece and it was worth it. One day I'll go to L.A. and paint huge murals with Retna and never freeze again.

Of course Donovan noticed my paint-stained hoodie, but it doesn't explain how he knew I had paint in my bag. I keep my locker locked my whole shift. How could he go snooping through my stuff? My black bag doesn't have a single drip on the outside. He'll forget about it. A few more make-out sessions with Jordyn, and Donovan won't even remember I exist. He won't get to see this hoodie again as a reminder, that's for sure.

I pull the handle on the donation bin and the hinged drawer swings opens with no resistance. I squeeze the hoodie close to me, the chemical smell of fresh paint lingering. I drop it into the drawer, and it slides into the bin like it can't wait to get away from me. I hope it keeps someone else warm and safe. The thing is full of good juju, as Mee would say. I stand by the bin for a moment and sign, "Thank you." My chest feels tight again, but I'm not out of breath. I'm not going to cry. It's a piece of clothing. No crying over clothes.

(๑_๑)

A crack of light shines from the doorway onto my bed. After a moment or two it grows wider and Mee stands there, silhouetted. She holds out a tub of coconut oil for me to take as she sits on the edge of my bed. I slide to the floor and sit at her feet. She reaches into the jar and warms up a chunk of the oil between her palms. I swivel around to face her so we can talk. Mee has this perfect smell about her. Maybe it's biology and we're all programmed to love the way our moms smell. Sandalwood and sage: she's always burning something in little trays or pots. Her acupuncture studio is full of these smells, too. They cling to her, following her from room to room. But above all, she smells like sweet coconut oil, and it's my favorite smell in the whole world.

"Wanna talk?" she signs slowly, hands glistening with oil. I stiffen and sit up. She saves this phrase for when I've messed up.

"What happened?" I throw my pointer fingers down.

"Nothing, nothing. Nothing bad." She rubs the oil into my hair, starting at the scalp and working her way to the ends. "Things calming down yet?" she asks.

"A little. It's fine." I tell her what she wants to hear.

"Come on, really?"

"Yes."

"Well, I'm——" She looks over my head at the door. "I'm

proud of you. I know it hasn't been easy." Mee braids my hair once it's saturated. I can treat my own hair, but there's something about the way she does it. My hair is glossy for a whole week afterwards. When I do it myself, I just end up staining all of my clothes.

I want to wrap my arms around her. I've been waiting for her to come back, for the wall to crumble down. It's getting chipped away, but I don't know what's doing the chipping. She isn't stubborn like me or Ma. Can't hold a grudge, always ready to move on. To forgive. All I manage is a shrug.

"Having to give up your art, that must be the worst of it." *Gulp*. "We should look into something for you to work on. Is there an art club? What about sets for a play? Or—"

"Yeah, maybe." I cut her off.

"Chin up, my jewel, this is only a valley." She drapes a towel across my pillow before she goes, knowing I would forget and stain the pillowcase when I sleep. Mee tells me to get some rest, kisses her finger, and touches it to my forehead. I fall back onto my pillow as she shuts the door. Taking her smell and the light with her.

I can't sleep. I want to sleep, but my eyes won't stay closed. They adjust to the darkness slowly, making it twice as hard to turn off my mind. My room seems so different in the dark. Cloaked in shadow, everything appears colorless and dull. I want to run down to my car, get my black bag from under the seat, and spray over every surface with the colors from my whale piece.

I blink my eyes and I see it, swimming in space, watching over me like some sort of spray-painted spirit. I sit up. There's no way I'm getting to sleep right now. I have to draw, I have to make something, to keep going. I don't want this moment to end. And who knows when I'll get to do something this big again?

Luckily, I have plenty of sketching supplies in my room. I just have to find them. I slip out of bed and a jolt of pain shoots up my leg. The culprit gleams in the moonlight: Jordyn's selfie stick. Her stupid fucking selfie stick that she insisted we buy from Chinatown. She spent all day waving it around, taking picture after picture, as if we didn't grow up in the city. I hate looking like a tourist.

Afterwards, she came over and binge-watched a bajillion hours of *Gossip Girl* reruns while I sketched in my B-book. I guess the novelty of the selfie stick wore off quickly, considering it's still here, lying in wait for the right moment to sneak up on me and bite. Well, this is the last time she hurts me.

I shuffle around in the dark, looking for any trace of Jordyn's presence. Anything left over from when I thought having a best friend meant something. Something big. But now I know better. It's better to keep to myself, not to trust anyone, not to care. Jordyn was only thinking of herself when she got me expelled, and now it's time for *me* to be the selfish one.

I find a pair of her hoop earrings and the old phone case that I tagged for her before she upgraded. I take those and the selfie stick and stuff them all in my empty Doc Martens shoe box. I remember her hoodie out there in my car, and I can't stand the thought of it being with Lee one more second. The hallway is dark and my parents are asleep, so I seize the opportunity to go and get it. I don't even bother putting shoes on. I want this finished.

On the way back up the stairs I spot one last friendship

artifact, a photo-booth strip we took in the lobby of a movie theater. I don't even remember what movie we saw, but we were so excited to try out those fancy new closed-caption glasses. It was incredible. The glasses made us feel like we had a superpower: finally we could go to any movie, at any time, and not have to worry about whether they were going to use captions or subtitles. We looked like futuristic sci-fi nerd-bots, but it was amazing. We just had to take some pictures with the glasses on before we returned them. I swipe the strip and head upstairs.

Everything goes into the box. I take a charcoal pencil from my dresser and mark every side with a giant X. All my ex–best friend junk goes into the X-box. I place the lid on top and it feels like I can finally put her out of my mind. She's just some girl now, like anyone else. It's done. We're over. No more besties, no more friends.

(屮° 口°)屮

Finley dominates the horizon as I pull onto Taylor Street. The auditorium is unmissable. It looks a lot like a whale, huge and blue, with the right side angling upward like a tail. I tried to capture a hint of it in my mural.

All the little fishy cars pull into the parking lot for another day of sink-or-swim. I can't tell which I'm doing anymore.

I didn't have time to do my history homework last night, so I decide to nap in my car until 9:15, when second period starts. I'll tell Casey I had car trouble, hit traffic, anything. I recline the seat and catch a glimpse of YP in my rearview, crying across the parking lot. It makes me feel nervous. I don't want to see her this upset, but I'm not trying to butt in. It's not my business. I can see her shoulders heave forward. Some other girl walks right past YP, not even bothering to stop and see what's wrong. YP doesn't let up, and my stomach turns. *Fine*. I lace up my boots, grab my stuff, and head over.

She's in some sort of argument with Kyle Fucking Stokers. *Shocker*. I hang back and try to get a feel for what's going on, but they're talking too fast and I can only see their profiles. I walk around the next row of cars to get a better angle. There's a lamppost there that I "casually" stand behind.

Snow starts to fall and creates a little halo around YP's blond crown. Her legs must be freezing in her signature yoga pants, but her feet are probably toasty in those sheepskin-lined boots. How could anyone fight with someone crying so cutely? But there he is, face red and scowling.

". . . not my problem," I catch him saying. She stares up at him with glossy cheeks, and he doesn't even blink.

"You said you——-————-——I got back." Snow and spit obscure her lips. She tries to say something more, but KFS cuts her off.

"What——-——————about it?"

"Everyone will——-" She covers her face with her hands and sobs.

"Jesus, stop crying. . . ." He looks around, embarrassed. His plea doesn't help: YP heaves even harder into her mittens. *Enough's enough.*

I walk quickly. The falling snowflakes prickle at my nose, and I blink furiously to keep the flurries out of my eyes. I aim straight for his back and "accidentally" slam into him. He hits the ground with what I imagine is a gratifying thud.

"Oh! Sorry! I didn't see you!" I sign to him, neither caring that he doesn't understand me nor offering to help him off the ground. I take YP's arm and I lead her into the mouth of the whale, leaving Kyle Fucking Stokers for the sharks.

"T H A N K S," she fingerspells. I show her how to sign it.

"What was that?" I point back to the entrance of the school as we make our way to history class.

"Long story," she mimes. I'm getting tired of this answer.

"Well?" I prod.

"Not now." She looks down at the floor when she signs the words. She doesn't turn down the hall with me for class.

"Come on!" I wave.

"-———-my locker," she mumbles. Making excuses to leave me behind. "Thanks———-Julia, it———-a lot." She looks into my eyes, hoping I'll get it and leave her alone. She doesn't actually need me. "Go, go! I'll be right there," she says as the bell rings. Of course she wasn't.

"You haven't seen her? She wasn't in gym, either," I sign one-handed, munching on a deli pickle.

"No, maybe she went home early." Casey unwraps her sandwich and folds up the foil into a perfect square.

"Before first period is way early."

"It is." Casey tries not to smile. Seeing me get along with someone else has her almost giddy. I don't know what she's over the moon about; she had nothing to do with it. Obviously, YP and I aren't close enough for her to tell me what's *really* going on with her. Considering she just vanished without out a good-bye after I got her away from KFS this morning.

"Whatever. She can do what she wants." It's not like we're real friends or anything. I ball up my own foil and napkin and stuff them into the brown paper bag.

"I'd tell you to bring her her history homework, but I'm not sure she'd receive it," she says.

"What's that supposed to mean?"

"You've been kind of a slacker lately, haven't you?" she says in that joking-but-not-really-joking way. I give her the side-eye on my way to the trash bin. *Get your own life.*

When I'm back at my seat, Mr. Katz is there, talking to Casey.

"Good news!" she signs.

"Hi," he waves. "I . . . uh . . ." He looks over to Casey and back at me.

"You're fine," I sign to him. "What's up?" Casey might be interpreting behind him but he looks at me when he talks. I love this.

"A spot opened up in my class."

(; ⊙_⊙)

It's the middle of November and I can't believe how the snow is piling up. I love when it flurries; there's something magical about it, like little stars falling all around you, getting caught in everything. Anyone who says otherwise is a bore. The only thing I hate about the snow is the cold. I'm amazed I didn't freeze to death out at the baseball diamond last night. I almost put on *two* bras this morning to make up for it.

Despite the day's drama, it ended perfectly, so I drive the long way home to get a celebratory sighting of my whale piece. I wonder how many people have driven past it today; if I keep this going, I'll be getting up in Greenlawn in no time. My rep will skyrocket. My hands get sweaty when I turn onto Cobblestone Avenue with the field up ahead. The snow fades the grass a minty green. I drive slowly: I want a nice long look at my piece. But there's something off about it. I only used what I had left: gray, blue, tan. So what is that big pink—

What. The. Hell.

I squint. It must be the snow playing tricks. I need glasses, right? No, it's there, almost winking at me as I drive past. This couldn't be the same poser from before, that scribble skeleton. This? This took planning. Those bones could have been cut from a textbook and pasted up, they're so precision-perfect.

Whoever it is must be freakin' fast as lightning. They had time to spot it, grab their gear, and bomb my piece all in the

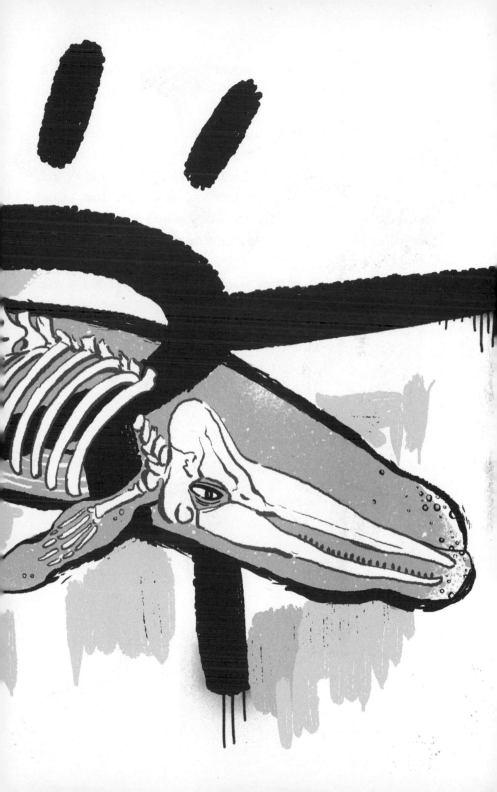

same damn night. I never would have pegged Greenlawn as having throw-down streets. It's all white-picket, seasonal-flag, Prius territory.

Haven't seen a lot of graffiti, at least nothing special. Yet as soon as I do some real writing, try to get up with my new name, someone's gonna just slash it like that? I didn't diss anyone. I'm not painting over anyone's work this time. I can't imagine where around Finley is considered "turf." I haven't heard of beef springing up like this since I was tagging in Queens.

Fine. If that's how they want to play it, get ready for war.

(//・_・//)

How am I going to buy paint? All that's left is a few colored puffs of air hanging tentatively in my school locker. Starting a war on Empty is a shit position to be in. Looked into the P.O. box. No one will ship paint to one. I'm not old enough to open one anyway.

Those damn bones. If they looked crappy, I could rest easy; I'd have the upper hand. But they were above and beyond—not someone I'd want to take on, normally. I don't know what pisses me off more, that they ruined my whale or that they might have made it look cooler. Dick.

The Internet hasn't offered much help in my paint-acquisition research. I'm about to call it quits for the night when my inbox goes: (1). It's a video hangout invite from YP. I throw my quilt over all the papers on my bed and take a quick glance in the mirror across the room. My hair has tangled itself into a nest on my head where a bun used to be. I yank out the hair elastic and shake out the tangles.

I've made it worse. I spot my red beanie poking out from under the bed. *Perfect*. Hair tucked neatly underneath, I hit Accept.

. . .

"Hi!" she waves. I wave back.

"I sign now okay?" She moves her hands slowly, but she gets it all.

"It's okay," I type into the box.

"No!" She pinches the air. "I want sign you one T H I N G." She's determined.

"OKOK."

"Sorry I go home today. Today not good day." I can tell she's rehearsed. "I thank you for today, and you very nice to me, and—" I'm relieved when she catches her super-serious face on the screen, and we both start laughing.

jjjjjulia: Aaaaaaaaanywayyyyy . . . .

HeadsNHearts: Did i miss anything good?

jjjjjulia: nah. Mr. Clarke needs trim his damn nose hairs already.

HeadsNHearts: lol

jjjjjulia: so . . . what happen????

HeadsNHearts: Ok well. so me and Kyle went out like, all last year

jjjjjulia: rough.

HeadsNHearts: it wasnt. we were so good together. real cute and stuff.

90

jjjjjulia: im sure you were the cute one.

YP rolls her eyes in the video window, before returning back to the keyboard, determined.

HeadsNHearts: i got him, i knew him. like, the REAL him. we were so REAL.

jjjjjulia: Kyle???!!

HeadsNHearts: I thought he was . . . ugh im such an idiot.

jjjjjulia: >:(

HeadsNHearts: okok long story short, he broke up with me when I got fat.

I take my hands off the keys and look at her. Really look at her. I've never been a person to use *fat* as an ugly word. It's something you either are or aren't. Deaf people aren't really shy about truly describing a person. It's not an insult; it's the way something is. I imagine Ma asking me about her, how would I describe YP? I'd probably use the words *shiny* and *blond*. She's big and beautiful. So what the hell?

jjjjjulia: what a dickhole.

HeadsNHearts: He isnt!

jjjjjulia: ಠ_ಠ

HeadsNHearts: I used to be really skinny and it turns out that was super important to him.

She's getting upset, her eyes tinting that wet shade of pink right before a tear squeaks its way out. Time to change the subject. I can't handle watching her cry over KFS twice in one day. I wave at the camera to get her attention before going back to my keyboard.

jjjjjulia: Some good news today

HeadsNHearts: Really?!

YP looks relieved to not have to go on.

jjjjjulia: got in Mr. Katz class!

HeadsNHearts: you deserve it!!! i wanna see your stuff

jjjjjulia: why?

HeadsNHearts: i think itd be good. Like how blind people are good at music!

jjjjjulia: um. i gotta go.

ಠ_ಠ

The still life in Room 105 has changed since my last visit. If my heart could sink any lower into my body, it would. All drapery, all the time. Couldn't I start off with something easier? I look over to the podium and my pear drawing is still up on the wall beside it. My nerves settle a bit.

Some students are already setting up their supplies, intensely staring down the grand array of cloth. Mr. Katz has suspended some of it from the ceiling with crystal-clear fishing line, purple and red ghosts drifting over the table. Underneath is a scarf draped over a sheet draped over a chair. The scarf lies inconspicuously among all the other flashy fabric, plain gray wool, nestled in like a little cat taking a nap.

That's where I'm starting.

Mr. Katz appears in the doorway, tote bag over his shoulder, wavy black hair smoothed into place. There's a one-inch pin pinned to his (blue?!) breast pocket, but he's too far away for me to see what's on it. He pulls a record out of his tote bag and puts it down next to the record player.

"Start when you're ready, guys." He looks out over his class. Some kids, sketchbooks closed, continue on with their conversations. What are they doing in here if they're just gonna goof off? Mr. Katz taps me on the shoulder and puts a sheet in front of me. My name is typed on top in nice bold letters:

JULIA

We're starting a new still life this week, take your time with it. I suggest you start off with quick gestural drawings to get yourself familiar with the setup and build up from there. This week we will work in pencils and charcoal and next week we will move on to color.

He stays to make sure I understand; I nod and smile. His pin has George Harrison's face on it. Casey butts in and starts talking.

"That was so thoughtful of you." She points to the hand-out. "I'm Casey, Julia's interpreter."

"Right, right! I forgot, I'm sorry." He extends his hand and she takes it in hers. "Andy. It's nice to meet you." They shake hands a little too long. I have to think of something to say so I can get Casey's hands away from him.

"Where's the sharpener?" I ask, and she obediently interprets for me. Ugh, I'm letting her show off. He does that thing again that none of the other teachers have grasped yet: he doesn't tell Casey where the sharpener is. Instead he looks right at me and points over to the wall.

When Casey is around, people don't bother looking at me when they talk—they look at her. When I sign, people watch her and wait for her to tell them what I'm saying. It's all I can do not to wave my arms and direct people to *look at me, I'm HERE*. I thank him and take my 5H pencils over to the sharpener.

He goes back to the record player and puts the needle down on the record he took out of his tote bag. I don't know or care what it is all that much. I zero in on the little scarf-cat nestled in the folds. This is going to be tough. Again, I look over at my pear still life, and I notice for the first time how poor the drapery looks.

Did he pick this still life on purpose? *Not everything is about you, Julia.* I decide to start with a blind contour of the scarf, sheet, and chair. I put my pencil down on the bottom left-hand corner and lock eyes with the still life, trying not to peek at the drawing, not allowing my pencil to break contact with the paper. It's one of my favorite ways to warm up, really get my eyes working.

I feel the rough texture of the paper under-neath through my superhard pencil. I try to keep my arm motions as fluid as the cloth looks. I'm in the zone, that place between here and my head. Tuning everything out except every fold and crease. Every wrinkle dangling in front of me and . . .

It's awful. I look over to the girl sitting next to me. She's shading in a nice deep shadow, perfectly capturing the drape hanging from the ceiling. Ugh, she's good. I squint over at the kids who were chatting earlier and even their drawings are in better shape than my mess. I start over.

It's okay. That was only my first try. I'll do one more blind contour and I'll be nice and warmed up. Pencil goes back down to the bottom left of the page, eyes focus once again on the mountain of folds in front of me.

Garbage. What was I thinking, begging to be in this class? I look out the window. The snow is still falling steadily: why aren't we drawing that?

"Need help?" Mr. Katz points to my book while Casey stands next to him. I timidly nod.

"Folds are all about gravity." He points to the highest drape and lets his finger trace along the outline in the air. "Starting at the bottom will only make things more difficult for you." Casey is mesmerized. So am I. "Try sketching out the whole shape first. Fill in the details later. Don't be so hard on yourself—" He stops and asks, "How do you sign your name?"

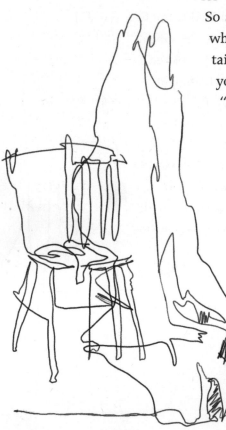

He doesn't get it right the first time; he has trouble with the hand shape. I take his fingers in mine. His hands are rough and dry. Mine are much warmer than his— it's either the coldness of his hands or the contact alone that sends a chill up my arm. I show him how to sign my name. Then he signs it himself, and this time, it's effortless.

"I love the name Julia. It's the title of my second favorite Beatles song." He smiles.

"You like the Beatles?" Casey interjects. "My favorite is 'P.S. I Love You.'"

"Oh, that's -———- -——-!" Mr. Katz says, turning away from me. They're off, chatting about the Beatles. I'm left in the dark because Casey has stopped signing.

The Beatles ruin everything. Everyone goes on and on and on about them: how revolutionary they were, how they'll never go out of style. People have asked me how I've been able to live without knowing what "Blackbird" sounds like. They give me that pity-face and say, "I don't know what I would do if I could never hear a Beatles song." I can tell you what you would do: you would get on with your life. I don't see what all the fuss is about. It's a band. Paul McCartney is old as hell. People put so much emphasis on music when I tell them I'm Deaf—like, without it, my life must not be as rich or full as theirs. Or they tell me to watch videos of people signing "Imagine." Barf. It's the same sort of shitty comment that YP let fly last night. It's either pity or fascination.

I give Mr. Katz a pass, though, because my third attempt at the still life was worlds better than my first two. That, and I didn't know my name was in a Beatles song.

$$(;\_ \cdot)$$

Back at McDonald's, I transfer the black bag into my work locker. All of the secrecy feels pointless when my bag's empty. I'm still pissed I can't put a message out there to whoever is bombing my art.

I've decided to switch out the combo lock for one that locks with a key. Donovan asking about the paint nags at me. I don't think he would go through my stuff, but I don't actually know him all that well. I take out my visor, Velcro it under my ponytail, and lock everything else away. The key gets added to my key ring. I hook it to the same loop as my broken Eiffel Tower key chain. One day I'll go and bomb the alleys of Montmartre with C215.

From the locker room, through the kitchen, and up to my station, it gets hotter and hotter. Jordyn is standing in the drive-thru window, helping Donovan with something. He leans over and whispers into her ear.

I've never really wanted to be hearing. If I had the choice, I would choose to be Deaf. There's this sense of community. People care more, do more—at least that's what I thought when I was at Kingston. Now, I can see why Jordyn got her implant. I've never had that, that whisper thing, that let-me-lean-in-and-tell-you-a-secret-in-your-ear thing. Lots of people make a big deal out of first kisses and hookups. But I want *that*. I don't even need to know what the secret is, I just want to be whispered to, I want to feel breath on my ears. They aren't dead. They can still feel.

I don't care what he's saying to her; the fact that he gets to say anything to her is enough to make me upset. She probably doesn't understand him, either: she wasn't implanted as an infant, and it's not the magic fix everyone thinks it is. I *do* know that she's loving the attention.

Jordyn thinks I should get CIs, too, but it's . . . So. Much. Money. Even if we could afford it, I wouldn't even want it, or the hours and hours of aural and speech therapy that go with it. I just want someone who will whisper secrets to me and not care if I hear them.

The manager must have said something, because Jordyn leaves Donovan's side, giggling. She pats my shoulder as she passes me, as if I'm somehow part of her shenanigans. All through the evening rush, I catch them staring at each other, smiling. I do my best to ignore them while I funnel the salt sticks into their boxes.

At the end of my shift, I serve myself an enormous fountain Coke, a sugary prize for making it through their PDA-fest. I grab an equally huge box of fries after I see them making out in the locker room when I leave.

What's wrong with me? I don't give a shit about who Jordyn makes out with. Donovan and I wouldn't work. He chose her because she's easier—easier to get to know, easier all around. I'm not easy. Never have been. Donovan taking the easy way out says more about him than me. So why should I care?

I don't need anyone but Lee. Tonight should be the night. I should get my revenge up on a wall, make my move already. I work my best magic when I'm angry.

Lee has really warmed up—she's almost hot. Which is how I prefer the temperature. If I could, I'd keep the heat at home cranked to eighty-five degrees all the time. I'm tired of the lectures and arguments over the dial, so I layer up the sweaters. The sky threatens snow again, but it feels like Miami in here. Not that I've ever been to Miami. One day I'll do a huge piece on the Wynwood Walls with Kazilla.

I pull over in front of YP's house, bright white with a green door and little Japanese maple trees under the windows. The lights are on; it's not too late. I haven't made plans with her, but I decide to get out and knock anyway.

Wait. What if someone else opens the door? Do they know YP has a deaf friend? Do I ask if YP is home? Oh, God. They won't even know who YP is. Why didn't I take more speech therapy? Oh, right . . . hated it. I reach for my phone so I can write out some sort of greeting, but I've left it in the passenger seat. *Craaaap.*

"Good evening." One of the biggest men I have ever seen cracks the door open. Imagine if the Brawny paper-towel guy and that Bunyan guy had a baby that grew up, grew a mustache, and moved to Greenlawn. I wave hello, point to my ear, then to my mouth. I form the word *deaf* with my lips.

"Oh!———-Julia! Come———!" He opens the front door wide and firmly ushers me into the living room with a slap on the back. He turns and calls for YP, I assume, having a brief conversation with the ceiling. The whole house smells like cinnamon and apples.

"You———-—-———from—-———-slice rye?" He raises his eyebrows. I have no idea what he asked. Mustaches are the bane of my lip-reading existence. I give him one of my "Huh?" faces and he tries again. This time he gestures a bit. He makes a slicing motion across his palm and then points to his mouth.

Oh! He's offering me pie. If it's as good as it smells, I'll eat the whole thing. I nod my head enthusiastically. His smile's so wide it's a little frightening. I follow him into the kitchen.

He serves me up an enormous slice and produces a can of whipped cream from the fridge. He holds it aloft and raises his eyebrows. *Yes yes yes.* I nod my head again, and he piles it on.

This pie. This pie . . . this pie is no ordinary apple pie. With apple pie, I usually expect something tart, with nutmeg, sugar, and cinnamon. Basic stuff, still delicious. But *this* pie, this pie tastes like vanilla, and instead of nutmeg, it's laced with oozing, gooey caramel. The top of the crust is sprinkled with sugar and . . . salt, of all things. It is art.

YP bounds into the kitchen in these knitted slippers with little pom-poms dangling from the top.

"You——more pie?" She playfully punches Mr. Brawny on the arm.

I sign to her, "Best best best pie!" Then I realize she asked *him* about it. I look ten feet up at him and mime: "You made this?" I thought it would be YP's mom, maybe even YP herself. This lumberjack of a man making beautiful delicate pies never would have crossed my mind. Ever. He smiles and gives YP her own slice. When he smiles, I see the resemblance, he looks just like YP. An unmissable personality.

"New recipe,——-gotta—-——least a bite." He pushes the

plate in front of her before pulling down three glasses from a cabinet.

He fills each glass with milk, ruffles YP's hair, and takes off down the hall. I can feel each footfall.

"He's always————————new flavors." YP dips her finger in some of what's dripped onto her plate and licks it off.

"Is it his J O B?"

"—started——summer. So what's up?"

Good question. Her dad and his dessert melted down my fury like ice cream under the heat lamp at work. I almost didn't care why I drove here in the first place.

"Are you OKOK?" she asks, after waiting nearly a minute for an answer. She tilts her head with genuine concern.

I down my glass of milk. It's thick and creamy, so much better than the skim that Mee makes us buy.

"Go out with me for a minute?" I point to her, then me, then the door. I pinch the air, point to my wrist. And hope she understands.

"Lemme ask." She skips off in the same direction as her dad, her blond bun dancing behind her. I rinse my dishes in the sink. She comes back holding her brown sheepskin boots and trades her slippers for them.

"He————back in thirty. That work?"

"Perfect."

"You told me a S E C R E T. Can I tell you one?" She's nervous about me signing (more like pointing) while driving. I don't watch my hands when I sign, and I keep one hand on the wheel. *Don't worry so much, YP. You're all right.*

"What happened? What is it?———about———
art class, or—" When she's excited, she talks so damn fast.
I shake my head, and wave my arms to cut her off.

"You'll see," I mime.

We make the turn for Cobblestone Avenue, and the scoreboard comes into view. I pull over. My headlights illuminate
my work *and* the work of my rival. I point. First to the painting, then to myself.

"What?" She looks confused.

"I (spray-paint motion) that."

"That—that's yours?" She covers her mouth, although it
looks more like her eyes might pop out of her head than her
tongue. I nod. She studies the scoreboard, her eyes tracking
back and forth and back again. She looks at me timidly. "Is—
—why———-—- expelled?"

I nod and pull out my phone.

> **JULIA:** I made a huge one on the back of the gym
>   at my old school.
>
> **YP:** They caught you?
>
> **JULIA:** Yeah duh.
>
> **YP:** So you still do it?
>
> **JULIA:** Obv

She types into her phone but she keeps deleting and
starting over. She looks at the whale again before finally
sending.

YP: its good. I like the different styles.

I can tell she's reaching for the compliment. I'm sure she's never so much as ended up in detention, let alone broken a law. It's kind of fun to feel like I might be corrupting her.

JULIA: The styles is my problem.

YP: Doesnt look like a problem.

Hah! Yeah freaking right.

JULIA: I not do it.

YP: I thought you said you did do it.

JULIA: I not do the bones part.

YP: Who did

JULIA: Not 100% sure on that one yet.

YP: You dont know???

JULIA: No its like some sort of turf war thing.

YP: War?

JULIA: They did this to my work. Now I need
    answer back somewhere

YP: So you take turns.

JULIA: And its my turn.

YP: But . . .

JULIA: ?????

She doesn't look at me, only at her screen, or the field. She doesn't seem excited by it. Maybe it's not her thing, but it's mine, and for some reason I want her to at least try to understand.

YP: Why does it have to be a war?

w(@ 。 @;)w

The drapes are looking very drapey in Advanced Art Studio. They loom overhead, taunting me with their highlights and shadows. The folds seem to have multiplied, thousands of little wrinkles and creases mock me: "*real* artists draw drapes." Today we start color versions of the same still life. Mr. Katz puts on a record at the beginning of class again, but this time he props up the sleeve so the class can see. It doesn't have the name of the musician on the front.

The cover is a painting, really rough brush strokes—I'm going to guess in oil paint by the way the colors mix up. It's a man's face. I'm not sure if it's the performer or not, but it's not painted in a very realistic way. Thick gray outlines, a big flat light blue nose.

There's a debate going on about it. I look over to Casey, but she's preoccupied with participating in the argument, rather than clueing me in. Katz keeps laughing and smiling at her. From what I can piece together, the guy across from me with the long brown hair and holey black T-shirt has a bad opinion about whatever is playing. A lot of the other kids are chiming in, too.

Casey tells him to get to his artwork . . . and something about the history of music? Mr. Katz finally steps in and lifts the needle, puts it back down on the same record, and says, "———listen———-next track."

The drama stops; everyone takes a moment to consider the song change. So much fuss over a song . . . aren't we in *art* class? Shouldn't you all be drawing? The next song seems to placate the room. Black Shirt closes his eyes, and nods along to the beat.

Mr. Katz comes over to me and kneels down so we're on the same level. He speaks at the perfect speed for lip-reading. Everything about him radiates a Zenlike calmness. "Did I show you where the paints are?"

I shake my head "no" and follow him over to one of the large wooden cabinets lining the back wall. He swings the door open, revealing an assortment of supplies. A box labeled "Oils," a box for acrylics. I pull out boxes one by one; dinged-up, dirty tubes fill each to the brim. Some of them must be empty, maybe only one squeeze of pigment left inside. Most are so caked with dry paint, you wouldn't even know what color you were picking out.

Underneath the paint boxes, there's a shelf full of pastels and colored pencils, followed by a shelf of watercolors. Dozens of little clear plastic trays stacked up and crammed into place. Under the watercolors there's one last shelf, and on it is an old plastic milk crate packed full . . .

Of spray paint.

I grab a tray of watercolors and turn away as fast as I can. I won't give it a second glance, won't risk being caught scoping the merchandise. At the sink I pick up a jam jar and fill it with water, take three brushes from the coffee can, unroll some paper towels, and head back to my seat.

Mr. Katz closes the closet. It doesn't even lock. Casey is standing in my line of sight for both the closet and the still life. I shoo her aside. *Don't even think about it.* I'm above stealing. *Where else am I going to get it?*

I dip my brush into the water, swoosh it around a bit, and dab the excess water on the paper towel. I rub the brush into the red first, getting the pan nice and wet. I'll start out with light colors since I don't really know much about watercolor painting. I grabbed the paint without thinking.

Another jam jar gets placed next to mine, and Mr. Katz calls Casey over to interpret.

"Two glasses keep the colors from getting muddy," he instructs. "One for cleaning your brush, one for adding to washes." Casey has obviously been practicing her art vocabulary. She doesn't skip a beat.

"Thanks." I smile. He moves on to the girl across from me; she's attempting to thin out acrylic paints with turpentine.

My eyes dart back to the closet again. *Stop looking!* But it's like I have X-ray vision and I can see right through the door. The cans sit there, unused. Collecting dust. Begging. I pull my eyes away from the closet and back to the cloth. I can't steal from the one teacher who's reached out to me. That's just bad karma.

I'm sitting cross-legged in my chair. The bottom foot hums with pins and needles—I miss my big armchair. I've started by painting general shapes again. Watercolor paint is trickier to work with; you can have too much water and get gloppy textures, or not enough water and end up with scratchy strokes. Not like spray: beautifully opaque, spray performs exactly as you'd expect all on its own. No water or thinners required. With the right caps, you can achieve a lot of range, too. I'm thinking about doing a stencil piece as my next move. Stencils can be stunning. Elevated. Next level.

I realize I'm staring at the paint cans in the closet. *Wait. When did I come over here? I don't even remember getting out of my seat.* I grab a few colored pencils from the top shelf and book it like mad back to my spot.

Casey waves: the bell rang. Class is over. Mr. Katz shows me where I can put my work to dry, a big rack next to the record player. I pick up the album and flip it over.

Bob Dylan—*Self Portrait.*

"It's a good—" He crosses his arms as he tells me, "I'll make you a copy."

I laugh and roll my eyes. Casey taps her foot in the hall. I close the door behind me on my way out. *Another door between me and that stash.*

$$\psi(o\ o\ )$$

Clicking on my paper lamp after school, I decide to figure out the paint later. Gotta plan out the piece first: I'm finally going to tag the underpass. I crouch down next to my armchair and grope around underneath it. I have my B-book Velcroed under there.

If I sketch or plan anything that has to do with graff, I put it in here. Not in my piles of regular sketchbooks, not on fly-away pieces of paper. They all go in here, in my bible, in my little black book. And I have some real work to get to.

So how do I retaliate? This will be *my* art. I consider doing one lone pear, but I scrap that quick. That's for Katz. What says ME? What says JULIA? What says HERE? It has to be all those things. It has to be *me* on that wall.

I flip through some magazines, hoping lightning will strike, but there's not a cloud in the sky. No one in the pages of *Nylon* is like me. I'm a fingerprint, an anomaly, a snow-flake. Indian, Deaf, girl, two moms. You couldn't make this shit fit in the pages of those glossy mags. I think about the curtains, the paint, the smell of Room 105. I think about the Zen being that is Katz, and his hypnotic red plaid. And I re-member "Julia."

I crack open my laptop and search for the lyrics to the Beatles tune I was unaware of. I wrote off the Beatles long ago, mostly because they're all over the map. I can't figure out what sort of music they play. A bunch of songs are all about holding hands and loving and *I love her* and *does she love me* and *she loves you,* blah blah blah. And then you have songs that are, like, some sort of country song about a bar fight with some raccoon guy, and another song about another guy who goes around bashing people with hammers? One of their songs goes on and on about doing it in the road and that's it. That's the whole song.

Someone explain the appeal.

Anyway, I figure if my name's in a song, maybe I can use it. Might as well see. I find a link and pull up the lyrics. I scroll through the lyrics pretty quickly, and I have to scoff. *Seashell eyes? What?* For some reason I read them again. And again. And again. The lyrics repeat in my head, and I try to imagine how they would play out loud. The words are too dreamy to be a rock song. I repeat them even slower. I pick up my pencil.

The words don't leave my head as I draw. My brain is pre-occupied with the words and my hand takes over. *Am I hypnotized?* Line after line, the drawing starts to come together. Three colors. *Where's my X-Acto? Where's my poster board?* The song in my head plays on as I start tracing out the first image.

I know it doesn't look like much yet, but it will. I cut away all the pencil, making lace out of paper. I love this part just as much as all the rest of it. The methodical, unrushed part. The quiet creation before the spray-paint storm. I have the words memorized. *Is this what it's like to get a song stuck in your head?* I start working on the second board when the overhead fluorescent lights flash. I shove everything under my armchair before running over to the stairs. It's Ma again.

"Everything okay?" She's checking in, but she doesn't invade my space. It's the first time since Kingston she hasn't just walked downstairs without a heads-up. It's a relief and I mean it when I tell her, "Perfect."

(˘‿˘)˘‿˘ C)

YP slams down her lunch tray and a few stray chips fly onto the table. Casey is thrilled to get to interpret our lunchtime conversations. Sometimes she tries to drag other kids into it, but YP is the only one who sticks around.

"What's wrong?" Casey beats me to asking her. YP ignores Casey and stares at her lunch tray.

"Everything all right?" Casey pushes. I hope Pants comes up with some sort of answer, because Casey could go on like this forever.

"Well, no. Officially lost my chance at Cheer this year."

"You actually like that stuff?" I pull my hands away from my chest, touching my middle fingers to my thumbs. Casey interprets for us.

"I liked having lots of friends." She doesn't make eye contact with either of us. Her eyebrows are hidden under her bangs. I can't tell if she's upset or angry. I'd be neither; those girls weren't her friends, not real ones anyway. What kind of friend texts you insults, abandons you?

"Can't you at least try out?" Casey urges.

"No." YP shoots me this look, one I recognize the meaning behind. She doesn't want to talk about it. I try changing the subject.

"Casey, you know that Beatles song, 'Julia'?"

"Of course! John Lennon wrote it for his mother." She

113

cleans her round glasses on her scarf, shining proudly. She loves whcn I ask her questions. Especially if they involve her opinion on something.

"His mom?" I put my thumb in my chin and my fingers stick up, making the sign for *mom*. "But it's a love song!"

"You can love your mom!" Casey objects. YP and I both crack up.

"People don't write *love* songs for their moms," YP chimes in.

"Why not?" Casey asks.

"Weird," I sign. "It's weird."

"*Tsk*." Casey puts her glasses back on, rolling her eyes. She makes the sign for *bathroom* and leaves. She'll meet up with me next period, no matter how much I wish she would get lost in the halls.

I text YP.

JULIA: Why cant you try out?

YP: Everyone hates me now.

JULIA: For for??

YP: Same reason Kyle dumped me.

JULIA: 凸(>皿<)凸
Screw them try out anyway.

YP: Why? So I can be humiliated?

JULIA: You care too much

YP takes her tray, untouched, and dumps it in the trash on her way out. I know how she feels. This time I don't let her get away.

"Hey!" I use my voice to get her to turn around. The hall is empty; my voice is just for her.

"Sorry," she signs.

"It's OKOK," I sign back. "I understand."

The whites of her eyes are pink again: this must be really important to her. That, or she cries a lot.

"Come on." I walk in front of her down the hall. After lunch I have English, which I hate with every fiber of my being. And, shit, I've been trying. Trying to keep my texts to YP clear and understandable. Not falling back on the old texting habits I had with Jordyn. That's something I do miss, not having to watch my words when I type. Using whatever grammar I damn well please and not being called stupid or slow. I hate English. Hate. I'd have no problems ditching, but I'm the only junior with a babysitter. Sure, my teacher could *find out* I cut, but he wouldn't be able to leave class and *search the school* like Casey can when I don't turn up.

YP wipes her nose on her sleeve. I don't care, I'll deal with Casey later. *This is more important.* We turn down the art wing and make it to Room 105. I peek inside the long thin window and the room is empty, exactly like the first time I came here.

I open the door and motion for YP to follow. She looks around the art room and her shoulders drop. She exhales and starts bawling. I consider hugging her, but it feels weird. I never know what to do when someone is crying. Pat her on the head? I stare at the wall. It's covered in drawings of perfectly rendered cloth; they put my little pear to shame. YP slumps down into a chair next to me.

"I lost everything, all———, I thought———-——-be better. I———-I was better." Her lips are puffy and moist, but I get the gist.

"What happened? For real," I sign. She seems to understand.

YP covers her eyes so she doesn't have to look at me when she mouths very deliberately, "I—-sick—-getting better———gaining weight."

Oh. She looks over her hands to gauge my reaction. I pull out the seat next to her and join her at the table.

"I was alone. Before. I didn't———anyone. I—-skinny and suddenly I—-whole entourage." She sighs, a big breathy exhale from the bottom of her stomach. What good is an entourage if they don't really know you? If they don't really see you for who you are?

"So, I didn't want to, you know, get better. ————————was great—-———. And Kyle . . ." It's better to let her talk. I don't think she wants to hear my opinions about Kyle Fucking Stokers, or her fake-ass friends at the moment.

"He made me feel like it didn't matter. All———work—--——-counting, and pills, and walking, and everything wasn't important. ———I was more important."

"You are more important." Kyle and I actually agree on something.

"I went and got help and he———-text me and—-————————it wasn't———allowed. I got better, and I came back. And everything was so messed up. ———worse than before. Everything I loved is over."

The way she hunches over in her chair, the drapes soaring to the ceiling behind her, she looks like she has wings.

"I draw you?" I ask without asking. I pull out my

sketchbook and flip to a new page. Moving quickly, I take a box of markers from Mr. Katz's podium. I wish they were paint pens. We could use the fumes.

We sit in the empty room while I outline her figure. I thought YP was one of those girls who never shut up, the ones who blather on and on just for the sake of talking, who don't listen to what you're saying. It's always about them. Turns out YP likes it quiet, too.

I swivel the book around on the table to face her.

"This, this is, perfect." She's getting better at ASL every time she signs. She must be practicing. She's right, it looks great. I'm working in my real style: fast, loose, markers, colors. It's all me, and all her. I rip it out and give it to her. YP puts the drawing down in front of her.

"What about you?" she signs.

"What about me?"

"Tell me something. I want to know more about you." She waits for me to respond, but I don't know what else to tell her. I told her about my street art, what else is there? "What about boys?" YP asks with a small smile.

"*Worst!*" I sign with the angriest eyebrows I can muster.

"S P I L L." Her eyes widen and she leans in.

And I tell her. I tell her about Donovan, which leads to Jordyn, and all her hearie boyfriends that last a month or two at a time. How it never bothered me before, but of course it bothers me now. About how it makes more sense for him to choose Jordyn anyway. I don't think she can understand half of the words, but she nods in all the right places.

"You were friends with her?" YP signs the word *friends* a few times with a scrunched-up forehead.

"I thought so."

"I don't know if——-friends with *you*," she says, assuming. I didn't lecture YP about her phony friends.

"But she was." I nod and sign. "She was my best friend." I think back to when Jordyn would sleep over and we would spend all night watching Bollywood movies, with Ma and Mee dancing around the living room. Jordyn would play along, but then make fun of me for days afterwards. I know Bollywood movies are silly, but they're mine. A part of me.

And then it sinks in: Is that what Jordyn is? Just a big faker? YP straightens up with wide eyes. She makes her hands into fists, and uses them to sign "shoes," then points to the door. We look around for a place to hide. I know all the closets are packed; there's no way we would fit in any of them.

"Quick!" She hops up on the still-life table and offers me her hand. I take it by instinct and she pulls me up to meet her. YP lifts up one of the hanging curtains and wraps it around us both. It reaches all the way down to the table, where it cascades onto the floor.

She looks over her shoulder, listening for the door to open. She holds a finger up to her lips, forgetting I'm not really one to make a peep. I wonder if the sound of my heart pounding in my rib cage is as loud to her as it is to me. Her eyes shift from the door to the other side of the room and back, her neck craned over her shoulder, for one of the longest minutes of my life.

"C L E A R?" I ask. Signing has its advantages.

"I think," she exhales, and starts laughing. We scramble out of the room as fast as we can.

In the hall, YP checks the time on her phone before rushing off to her AP calculus class. I should be walking to my next class with her, but I lag behind. After she turns the corner, I go back inside the art room.

I can't just steal the paint, right? I've never stolen supplies in my life. It goes against everything I'm about. My graffiti is more about the art, less about the vandalism. Stealing to make it happen? That's not art.

But no one is using it! It's sitting there in a cabinet untouched and unloved. How would we even use spray paint in class? Indoors? Maybe it was donated or something and Katz doesn't know what to do with it. If I don't take it, it's only going to keep collecting dust. And whoever is ruining my work gets to win our war by default.

I take three cans.

⊙＿⊙

"**Y**ou can't cut class and not tell me." Casey is furious.

"I was helping YP! It's not like there wasn't a reason." Some things are more important than proper sentence structure. Why don't teachers get that? Ninety percent of the time, fine, I'm there in class. Sometimes shit hits the fan, though, and we're supposed to ignore it?

"You're not understanding me—" she goes on. Damn, Casey, you're not even that old. Don't you remember what this was like? I tell her exactly what I think she wants to hear, but I can't help but roll my eyes as I do it.

"No, I understand. I have to go to class and try to be better and be brave, and if I don't start getting better at English I'm gonna make Deafies look stupid and—"

"What? No! I know your friend was upset. I saw her at lunch, too, and if you had asked me, I would have let you."

What?

"You make yourself look worse when I show up to your class and you don't."

Is this real life?

"Get it?" Her pointer finger flicks up at the ceiling. I'm so stunned I can barely nod.

"I told them you weren't feeling well, so let's go to the nurse and make it look right."

Casey, who are you?

121

((('д';)))

"Liar," Donovan signs. "You very liar." He grins. Jordyn must be teaching him more signs. I don't know why she would bother.

"I've never lied in my whole life," I lie as fast as I can, and when he doesn't reply I puff my chest out and roll my eyes.

"You paint. You paint! I know." He signs some more then speaks. "Jordyn——me all———-it." If I wasn't sweating after my extra-long shift, I was now.

"I quit all that," I sign, dusting imaginary crumbs off my palms. "Finished with it."

My shoulders ache under my black bag. It feels like it's full of bricks, not paint cans.

"Liar," he signs again. He zips up his hoodie. The zipper looks like a spine, with a rib cage printed on either side of it.

"I gotta go." I point to the door and wave, fingers clenched around the straps of my bag. I can't get out to my car fast enough.

What's Jordyn running her mouth for? She knows the kind of trouble I could get into. As far as she knows, I've moved on from all that, anyway. So why would she go and talk to him about it?

The wipers clear the snow off my windshield. There's something stuck to one. Trash? It's yellow, like the burger wrappers inside Mickey D's. I stop the wipers and struggle, reaching out of the window, to grab it.

I wait until I'm home to inspect the note again. The snow has blurred the letters, but there it is, clear as day. This shouldn't be possible. I know it's my move, thank you very much. What I don't know is how the hell you know who I am. I shove the note in my pocket and start pacing on the sidewalk in front of our house. My footprints in the snow diagram the steps of some long-lost stress-induced dance called the Panic.

I feel sick, violated. I'm going to pass out; I need to lie down. This isn't just a major diss, it's a threat. It's *scary*. I can feel the sweat beading on my forehead. I'm hot, so damn hot. I lie on our little patch of lawn and let the snow fall on my face.

This isn't okay. This isn't happening. Out in the open, up on a wall, anonymous is one thing. This, though? On my car, *my* car. I'm aware of every flake that touches down and melts on my face. They know who I am. They know I'm Julia; they know I'm HERE.

I run through that night again and again as the snow collects in my hair and around my ears. I parked at least a mile away from the field that night. After I dumped my hoodie and walked to my car, I checked over and over again to see if anyone was following me. I took random streets on the way back, not the quick or easy route.

Who is it? Who could possibly be this offended by my work? Be so up on their game that they notice my graff right after it goes up. I decide to head to my basement command center and work through the fear. I have one last stencil to finish.

I slice through the poster board with a little more care this time. Ma and Mee are on one of their date nights, so I don't have to worry about them sneaking up on me. I can work and think. Every now and then my hand finds its way into my pocket and I wrap my fingers around the slowly disintegrating note. YOUR MOVE. *Oh, I'm sorry, am I not moving this along fast enough for you?*

The little cuts in the board shine like stars when I hold it up to the light to check my progress. I've been playing it so safe, and still I get caught. I guess I should be thankful it's a rival and not the cops.

How did Donovan know I had paint that day?

He saw my hoodie.

Is that enough?

He knows my car.

He has that hoodie. That skeleton hoodie!

Jordyn told him I *used* to spray.

What exactly does that prove?

Why did he bring it up tonight?

Where did he go on his break?

Does he have Post-its in his locker?

How does he know I'm a liar?

No. No way. I refuse to believe it. He's not clever enough— he's all looks. This sort of work takes brains *and* talent. He's with Jordyn, so what's he messing with me for? *Obsess much?* I thought I was the obsessed one.

Since when are you an artist, Donovan? You never said anything before. I guess you never said anything, period. Do you *like* me or something? Is that what this is about? Trying to play the same game as me? What else did Jordyn tell you about me? Did she whisper it in your stupid ear and you thought, OH, HEY, THAT'S COOL, LET ME GO AND MESS WITH HER ART, TOO, SINCE I CAN ONLY MESS WITH HER AT WORK. Goddamn it.

I roll up my stencils and venture out into the cold again. *My move.*

(ˆ) /占~~~~~

I'm on edge, and I don't like it. I should be buzzing, I should be driving down to the overpass high on sweet guerrilla endorphins. I'm ready. I have everything in place, my plan committed to memory, but I'm on edge.

How does he know I'm a liar?

The wind blasts through the tunnel, stinging my face. I thought to wear more layers this time, but I'm still freezing. I decide to put my piece up near the far exit of the overpass. The one-way street will give me some time to dash if I have to. I've learned some new tricks since my last bomb.

I slide the first stencil out of my bag's straps. Each stencil is cut from black poster board: nice dark camouflage, no giant white beacon in headlights. I use Sticky Tack to get it up on the wall. I do the tack at home so each stencil already has it in place. I peel the roll apart and stick it right on up. It always ruins the stencils but I don't keep them after finishing anyway. Rip 'em and ditch 'em.

Black can goes first. I shake it up and spray across the poster board. I have to get paint in every cut. The black on black on black makes it harder to see what I'm doing, and I waste paint going over the same spots more than I need to. The wall looks like a paint-eater anyway, so I keep the spray flowing. Doesn't matter if I run out, as long as it looks perfect.

The tunnel brightens up. *Car's coming.* I grab my bag, leave the stencil on the wall, and haul ass through the nearest exit. I toss my bag, and it lands behind a bush on the hill outside of the tunnel. I leap down in the frozen dirt, next to the bag.

No time to waste. On the ground, I prepare for Stencil Number Two, uncap the blue and holster the black. I lie back, and my breath forms little clouds above my face. Cars are going by, I can feel it but I can't tell if they're on the overpass or under it.

The sky is blanketed with heavy gray clouds. Every now and then a star is bright enough to peek through. Maybe it'll snow again soon, but I hope not tonight. On the other hand, if it snows, maybe people will stay home and I'll have enough time to finish. *Have I waited long enough?* My neck is freezing down here on the ground. I wait another full minute before I decide to dash back to the tunnel.

I rip down Stencil Number One. I try my best to get the cutouts on the second board to register in the right place, but it's okay if they're slightly off. I think it looks cooler that way sometimes. The Sticky Tack doesn't hold up too well in the cold, so I have to really press it into the concrete. I have blue ready to go. This time the lighter paint color makes it much easier to see if I've sprayed in the right spots. I double-check over both shoulders while I spray. The coast is still clear and I throw up the final stencil, the first two in shreds at my feet.

The final layer is the magical one for me. It's what makes the whole thing come alive. The highlights, the special moments, all happen on that last round. My arm and fingers shake. My right hand is frozen into that spray-claw shape so badly I worry that I won't be able to pry the purple can out of it. Everything aches, even though I haven't been at it all that long. Stencils don't care if I'm shaking, so no need to spray in a straight line.

I rip down the last stencil and ball all three up. I'll toss them in random trash cans on the way back to Lee. I take my Screaming Silver paint pen out of the front pouch and sign the piece. *HERE*.

(˘＿˘)

The still life is down in art class this week. Nothing is set up in the center of the room. Casey is already in the middle of a conversation with Mr. Katz (green flannel today) near the record player. When he sees me take my seat, he holds up a finger and grabs something from inside his tote bag.

"Here, I made—--copy." He slides a big used yellow envelope on my desk. I slip out the stack of papers inside and on top is a color printout of the Bob Dylan cover. I flip through the stack: there's a new page for the lyrics to each song. Katz has drawn little doodles in the margins: fish swimming, horses, hands reaching for things.

"I thought that—"

I cut him off with a wave, he doesn't need to say anything. I put my hands over my chest, one on top of the other, trying to keep in the warm feeling that's started to radiate there. I don't want Casey to interpret. I want Mr. Katz to understand me like I understand what he just did for me. It's hard to look him in the eyes; I felt something in me unlock and I don't want to share it. But if I want him to understand how grateful I am without words, I have to.

When our eyes meet, we both must look so worried, so serious, it's funny. I burst out into a laugh, and I'm relieved when he starts laughing, too.

"Thank you." I slide the pages back into the envelope and

tuck it away into my bag. *This is mine.* It's all for me. Then the guilt worms its way into my chest. Why did I take that paint? I immediately start thinking of ways to repay him. What would be an equivalent gesture? I can't really make him a mixtape, considering I don't know all that much about the art of it. Maybe my next piece, something with red, something—

Black Shirt hands out paper and Sharpies to everyone in the class. Casey takes her position as Mr. Katz starts explaining our next unit.

"For the next few weeks, we're going to be talking about street art." My ears are hot. There's no way he can know. I glance around the room, scanning faces to see if anyone else is flipping out. No, it's just me.

"I wasn't planning on doing this lesson until the spring, but I was inspired on my drive to school this morning."

Gulp. Katz saw the mural. He must have. He can't know it was me, I've been so careful. How many cars drove by when I was painting? It couldn't have been that many. It's just a coincidence, at least it inspired him. Stop blushing, you're only making it worse.

"Before we start, though, I need you all to promise me that you will practice your work only here in class."

"What's the point, then?" a girl with freckles asks.

"The point is to learn about a different art form, add more styles to our toolbox. Who knows? Maybe you'll be hired to paint a mural one day."

Aw, what a cute notion. Styles in our toolbox, and getting hired for murals? As if that's the same thing as real street art. Mr. Katz, I love you, but sometimes you're so corny.

"We're going to start out using our real names for our work here. No nicknames yet. So, first, I would like you to start experimenting with the letter forms of your name. Feel it out. Try not to rely on your pencils and only use the pen. You wouldn't get to erase in the real world."

True, that.

Tagging with my own name feels wrong. Even on a piece of non-incriminating paper, it feels off. *This isn't how it works.* You don't sit down with a Sharpie and write your name over and over. Well, I guess you sort of do. But definitely not in a room full of other kids all doing the same thing.

Ugh. My fingers get dappled in Sharpie. Dead giveaway. I'll have to try and explain this to my parents. *I swear, it's for class* probably won't cut it. Maybe Casey will back me up on this one.

When I tag, it's not about slapping my name on a wall. It's more than that. Right now, though? I'm not jamming out. I'm not going into that amazing, humming, buzzing trance that happens when I'm dreaming up new work. It's just my name, just paper. The *J* is ugly and the stupid *I* looks like another *L*.

Mr. Katz comes over and looks at my paper.

"Hmm. I thought --- ----- be good at this." Wait. Did he— or am I misreading lips again? How would he know? Some gossiping secretary who knows why I was expelled? Teachers want to act like they're above rumors and gossip, but I know shit spreads faster in the main office than in the cafeteria. He laughs to himself as he moves on to the girl sitting next to me.

BOOM! *I win*. I drive down Spring Road on my way to work. My fingers, still smudged with Sharpie, wrap around the steering wheel. My piece is still burning under the overpass, and, more important, untouched. Now this, *this* is real street art. Not some Sharpie doodled on poser-printer paper in art class.

This takes ovaries.

I wonder if Donovan has seen it yet. Maybe he's planning his next move, or maybe he thinks *I* haven't made a move yet. Whatever. Move made. *BOOM!*

I strut into work like a boss. Like a queen. Like a CEO. Like nothin's gonna bring me down. Check my swag, D. It puts yours to shame. Jordyn is already getting changed when I strut into the back room. I'm glowing and nothing she says is going to kill my buzz.

"I wanted to talk to you," she signs. I pull down my visor to avoid looking at her.

"Doesn't matter." My hands swipe back and forth.

"I think I'm getting serious with Don—"

"And?" I cut her off.

"Well, I need you to back off."

"Back off what?" I snap. I'm losing my patience with Jordyn and her demands. My conversation with YP replays in my head. Jordyn was a real friend, I didn't make that up. Right? I was always there for her—all she had to do was text. I remember bringing her chocolate shakes after a particularly dramatic breakup. We ate them with spoons on her fire escape, and she cried and I made jabs at her ex. That's not fake.

"Him. I know you like him. And he keeps talking about you."

"Why?" Seriously, I want to know. He shouldn't be talking about me to anyone. Did he tell you about our little war?

"I don't know, I don't really get it." Real nice, Jordyn. I wouldn't expect you to get it. "So, would you mind backing off? I'm with him now."

"Doesn't matter, okay? I'm over it, and I'm over you. You lost all your clout when you sold me out."

"I had to! They thought it was me!" she signs. Pathetic. She's never even taken an art class.

"No, they didn't. I stood up for you! I painted that wall for you! You were my best friend. What happened?"

"I wouldn't say *best* friend." She shrugs her shoulders like it's nothing. Like what she just said wouldn't slice through my heart.

"You're serious?"

"I mean, it's not like we hang out all that much, not unless we're working. Or at school. Don't make this weird, okay?"

"What was I to you?" My hands can barely sign the words, they're shaking with anger, with exasperation.

"Look, none of this has to do with Don—"

"Go bang every hearie in the world, for all I care." I cut her off furiously, my hands a blur, and I'm out the door. I might be burning bridges, but they're my bridges to burn.

The heat radiating off the fryer is welcome for a change; it's been so damn cold out. I should be standing here steaming mad after being passed over by Donovan, only to have him come back and invade my space after all. Does he like me or not? Is this about art or something else?

But all my anger is reserved for Jordyn. She stole my school and then she stole Donovan. They aren't worth the trouble anymore. I don't want her to think I'm on her thieving level. I'll back off, but I can't force him to do the same. The breakup chat we couldn't actually have plays out in my head.

We're both standing under the overpass by my latest. He looks so cute when he's defeated.

"What's wrong?" I ask.

"I can't do it, can't add to this. I wouldn't want to ruin it." *He might be holding back a tear or two.*

"That's all right. You tried." Pat, pat on the head.

"You're so much more talented than I am." Donovan looks at his feet.

"Maybe one day." Poor little toy.

"I'm sorry I ditched you for Jordyn. I thought she'd be easier to talk to, you know?"

"Was she?"

"Sure, but all she ever does is talk. She never listens."

"Shame that implant goes to waste, then."

"Hey, I was wondering—"

"Lemme stop you there, D. I'm sorry it's not going great

with Jordyn. *That's too bad. I'm also sorry your graff game is so damn weak. But I can't help you with that. You have to earn it. This could have been great. But I'm out."*

Drop the mic, etc.

Too bad I have to keep staring at the back of his head for hours. I wonder if I should leave a note on his locker: *Your move now.* Nah, let him find the underpass on his own.

I line up some fries under the lights, and start folding up little boxes for the next batch. I hate folding these things; they have such a freaking weird shape. No other box is shaped like a fry box. It's a singular thing, and it's annoying as hell.

Donovan keeps looking over his shoulder, except this time I swear he's looking at me, not Jordyn. She keeps filling soda after soda for him, back and forth, getting between us the whole shift. Every time she passes me she glares, or bumps into me a little too obviously while squeezing by. I'm surprised he's not in a diabetic coma by the time we leave.

Jordyn leans against my car, obviously pissed off, all toe-tapping and folded arms and a scowl visible from space. I can still smell the fries in the air, and the glow of the arches tints her skin a sickly yellow color. What happened? How did we ever end up like this?

"What?" I ask her before I even reach the car.

"You didn't let me finish," Jordan snaps.

"Finish what?" I reach past her and unlock Lee. She pushes against the door. I fight every urge to yank it open and send her flying.

"Knock it off." She touches my shoulders, forcing me to face her.

"You knock it off! I told you—"

"Shut up, Julia!" she signs and shouts. I back off. Let her say whatever she wants and after, I'll add her to my X-box and shove it in the back of my closet to rot.

"Do you like him?"

"I don't want to talk to you about boys."

"Please stop playing games, I need to know." She looks so hurt, and it kills me. Why doesn't she care about me the way she cares about him? I thought our friendship was worth more than some dude who works the drive-thru. I want to know why she sold me out, why she totaled our friendship but acts like it's still drivable.

"No. I don't like him." I lean next to her. We both stare off at some unknown point in the universe.

"Would you tell me if you did?" she asks without looking at me.

No.

"Yes."

"It's just that . . ." She starts pacing. "I don't know. I really like him. But he's dated a lot of girls at work, you know?" she asks, but it doesn't feel like she's actually asking me, or even talking to me. It's like she's trying to figure it out for herself while I'm on standby. It makes me miss YP and our talk in the art room. How she sat and listened, even if she had no idea what I was saying—she knew it was important. The more Jordyn rambles, the more upset I get.

"I guess it feels like, maybe he doesn't like me." She finally pauses and looks over to me, expectant. Waiting for me to comfort her, but I can't. I won't.

"Not everything is about you."

"Don't be so jealous," she says, laughing. But none of this is a joke to me, not even remotely. I swing open the car door, but before I can peel out in a fiery rage, someone zooms into the parking lot on a bicycle. It's YP.

"Are you OKOK?" I sign over the car to her.

"Fine, fine," she signs back, leaving one hand on the handlebars. She leans her bike up against Lee, and they look like they belong together. She's panting, hard.

"You rode all the way here?" I ask. It must have taken her hours.

"No, no. Bike, L I R R, and bike again," she signs, smiling and proud.

"What happened?"

"Not. Good." She takes her time, signing with purpose. Her eyebrows angled down, she shoots Jordyn some shade.

"Doesn't matter. What happened?" I ask again.

"What's going on?" Jordyn tries to get our attention.

"O V E R P A S S," she spells. "Not good."

{{p´ Д `q}}

tried to shake Jordyn, but she wasn't having it. If only YP could read my mind so we could talk without Jordyn butting in. Pants is getting good enough at sign; I just wish telepathy were the next step.

"Just tell me what happened," I sign to her. Jordyn must be having a conversation, out loud, with YP at the same time; YP keeps talking over her shoulder.

"Hello?" I wave.

"You want to tell her?" YP tries to sign out of Jordyn's sight. My need for info is trumping my beef with Jordyn. It's not like she can get me expelled from Finley. YP looks disappointed.

"Don't tell me you're painting again!" Jordyn squeezes between the seats. She's crammed in the back next to YP's bike wheel. The rest of the bike just barely fits in the trunk.

"She knows?" YP scowls from the passenger seat. Jordyn replies, but I have no idea what she says. I'm trying not to crash the car. It looks like they're arguing, from the few glimpses I catch.

I make the last turn onto Spring Road and there's a cop parked behind a pillar under the overpass. Lights off, he thinks he's being clever. He's not fooling anyone. Least of all me.

"Should we just drive through real quick, like normal?" I ask Pants.

"Wait!" She holds her arm out like she's protecting me from stopping short. Probably the first time a passenger has tried to protect the driver. A second cop walks across the underpass and gets into the cruiser. "We can't———see your car." Good catch, YP. I turn onto a side street, trying to make it look natural.

"D A I R Y B A R N?" I sign.

"Fine." YP's still upset.

Carefully avoiding Spring Road, Cobblestone Avenue, and Broadway, we snake through side streets, getting closer to our quasi-hideout. It's a long, winding drive, the silence punctuated by Jordyn and YP sizing each other up in the rearview mirror. I just want to see what happened on the underpass. Having my work painted over is hard enough to deal with; I can't be concerned with the possible hurt feelings of an ex-friend. I'll sort YP out later, she'll at least understand.

Dairy Barn stands tall and proud at the end of the road. I'm dying to know what those cops were up to. They didn't have a paint roller or anything, and cops don't usually do patch jobs themselves. We pull under the carport and YP leans over me to order a large iced tea. I pay with some quarters from the center console and we park.

"When did you start all this again?" Jordyn asks, shocked.

"I never stopped."

YP sits with her arms crossed, head leaning on the window. I nudge her shoulder and offer her the first sip of iced tea.

"Please! Tell me how it looks!" I beg.

"I think your move now." YP signs as best she can.

"What? No. That's not possible," I sign.

"Why not?"

"Because the guy who was doing it was at work with me all afternoon."

"*Donovan?!*" YP obviously says.

"Donovan did what now?" Jordyn butts in.

"Nothing," I tell her.

"Someone's been bombing her work," YP explains to Jordyn.

"Bombing?"

YP and I share a smile.

"It wasn't him," I say to myself more than anyone else.

"Then who?!" YP demands.

We all sit for a moment without saying anything. I really can't think of who it could be. Who knows me well enough? But the *who* isn't what's most important right now.

"Describe it," I plead.

"It's not— Don't— Don't get mad."

"What."

"It's not bad."

"I have to see it."

"Take my bike." She points to the backseat and pedals her arms. "We—-wait here— —-——car, right?" YP asks Jordyn, who only nods, dumbfounded by the whole situation.

I don't hesitate.

I pedal as hard as I can. Icy air burns my throat and stings my lungs. Puffs trail from my mouth like I'm a speeding steam engine. I don't bother with back roads. I'm just a girl on a bike, right?

I don't know what's racing faster, my mind or my legs. It's *not* Donovan. I was so damn sure. This means they still have a leg up. They know me and I don't know shit about them. My thighs burn as I push up the hill on Cobblestone. I haven't biked since I was a child, and I'm out of shape and practice. It doesn't help that YP is much taller than I am and my feet don't reach the ground. I wobble every time I have to stop.

The overpass is straight ahead, and thankfully, the pigs have moved on to haunt someone else. *For how long, though?* I take mental inventory. I don't have any paint on me, the Sharpie ink has faded a bit, but that's not proof of anything. I decide to risk it and bike through. That's what I came here for.

I slow down as I get to the entrance. My knees shake from biking, and from nerves. I try to swallow, but my throat is dry. Every breath stings. My chest heaves up and down. That dickwad. That asshat. That—

Genius. Goddamn it. YP was right. It's not bad. It's not even not bad; she was being kind for my sake. It's good. It's really fucking good. They elevated it. Brought it up to this whole new level of, well, art, I guess.

It was great before, but with two people working on different shifts, and more hours devoted to the piece, the more detailed and beautiful it became. Is it my move now? If it were up to me I would call this one finished. Clearly, they know their stuff.

They haven't stopped calling me out. It's obvious now that they really know me.

There should be a picture of this. But I know I can't take one, especially when the cops are snooping. Now I keep my phone and feed free of evidence. I stall another moment to look it over and really memorize it. I want this stuck in my head. Every shape, every line. The bones, the colors, the hearts, the hand . . . Wait.

The skeleton hand doesn't register up with the one I stenciled. It's pointing. Up. I look at the underside of the overpass. Nothing there. I walk the bike out of the tunnel, eyes locked on the pointing finger. I follow the bony index finger up again, and I see it. Screw you, Universe.

(´ω｀)

Maybe they *don't* know who I am. I smash my face into my hands, alone in the yellow glow of my paper lamp in the basement. There's no way in hell I can pull off a heaven piece like that. And for that matter, how did they? Climbing up a water tower? *Are you kidding me?*

Nothing makes sense anymore. I want to go back to Kingston, to my little school where no one challenged me, where I didn't have to worry about anyone butting in, where I was alone and happy with my work. Never mind that no one really noticed it there.

Back then, I'd have these fantasies of the cops trying to track me down and all the ways I'd elude them. People would notice my work popping up everywhere, would wonder if it's graffiti or art. Or if graffiti *is* art. I'd get up. I'd be a queen. All that good stuff. Now they're only snooping on my work because someone else had to come along and show off. Do your own work. Why drag me into it? *Am I not good enough on my own?*

I rub my eyes. This isn't worth crying over. *Don't be so weak*. I need more time, more supplies, more planning. There's no way my opponent is backing down, retaliating so fast and now one-upping me. It's not fair, I have school and parents and a job. I can't just drop everything to plan and paint in a day. I thought they knew me.

How do they know me? How am I going to get up to that water tower? *How? How? How?* I sink into my chair. I have to stop thinking about it or I'm going to lose it. My legit back-pack nags at me from the floor. I guess I could do some home-work for once in my life.

I pull out my illustrated Bob Dylan album and flip through the pages. The pages smell like firewood. I try to imagine Katz sitting there in his house, fire going, drawing in the margins. All that work, just so I could be included. I'm not sure I even deserve it.

Little fish swim all around one page, some realistic-looking with long flowing tails, some no more than goldfish-cracker-looking doodles. I laugh. I get up and grab one of my little staple-bound sketchbooks.

There was a sale on them last year and I stocked up. I have about five or six left, blank, ready and waiting for whenever I need them. I pick one with the kraft paper cover. I'll make him a book full of *my* language, poems in little drawings of hands and hand shapes. First, I'll draw his name sign.

I came up with it almost instantly. I can just picture the dark shade of green Casey will turn when she finds out I named Katz before her, too. But his was just too easy to come up with. I draw it spanning the inside cover and the first page. I don't like to waste any surfaces.

I have one of those cubby shelves stuffed with all sorts of art materials. Mostly dead markers, art sets from when I was a little kid, that sort of thing. I can't bring myself to get rid of any of it. I grab a shoe box full of gel pens/brush pens/Crayola markers and color in the lines. I leave parts uncolored. Too much color makes it heavy, or I get carried away and end up ruining it. I'm learning to hold back. That's

something else writing out there in the world has taught me. Being efficient means being minimal. Beauty can be found in only three colors.

I like this. I flip to the next page and the stress over my rival is only a slight hum in the back of my mind. The next sign I draw is the sign for *art*. It's a good opener. I do another full-page spread.

And another.

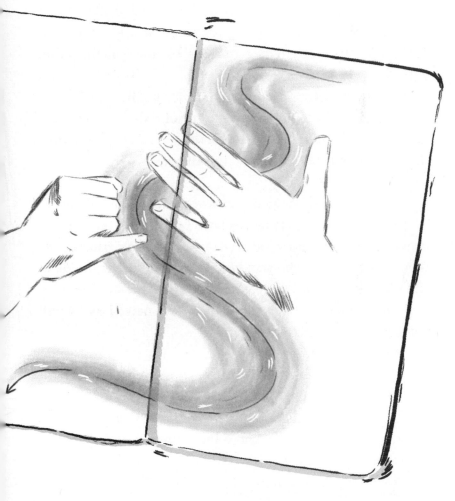

. . .

I keep sketching out words until the smell of pizza drifts downstairs.

We have a thing for comfort food in our house. It's sort of a family tradition. We'll order your favorite to celebrate for you, or if you've had a bad day. Twice, if you've had a bad week. Mee and I have the same favorite: Indian takeout from Rajdhani's. Ma is very into organic food and all that, but even she has a weakness. Hint: it's pizza. So when the smell of cheese wafts down to the basement, I know something's up with Ma.

I follow the scent upstairs and into the kitchen. Two boxes are stacked on the table next to a bottle of red wine and a tall-boy of Arizona Iced Tea. Mee pulls down three glasses from the cabinet and slides them next to the pizzas.

"What's the occasion?"

"We both had a rough day at work. Ma'll be home soon."

Damn, bad-day pizza means I can't fling open the box and chow down like with good-day pizza. It's their bad day, so they get to choose who should get the first slice. I decide to test the waters with Mee, get the art-class news out there.

"We're doing a street-art lesson in my new class." I pull out some paper napkins and plates.

"No, you're not."

"Well, not on the actual streets or anything."

"You're not joking?" Mee does not look excited.

"No, you know, there's a lot of cool history and stuff—"

"Of course there is. I know that. Don't you understand why that worries me?"

"You don't need to worry."

"It's like an alcoholic going to meetings at a bar." Screw this, now *I'm* having a bad day, too. I open the topmost pizza box.

"Hey! We're waiting!"

"I can't believe you compared me to an alcoholic."

"I didn't mean it in a bad way." Right. How else am I supposed to take that comment? As if taking a class on street art would force me to do it. I don't need a class for that. I'm not addicted: it's my *life,* not a bad habit that needs to be broken.

"Look, I think it's great you're learning about the history of graffiti and whatnot. I just want you to be careful." We both feel the door slam. Ma's home. She rushes into the kitchen, coat still on, and collapses into the chair across from me. She swings the pizza box around to face her and pulls out a slice.

"My day was hell," she signs while chewing. Another bonus of knowing sign: you can talk and eat at the same time without being totally gross. Mee takes Ma's coat off and rubs her shoulders before grabbing her own slice and joining us. The plates I brought out remain unused. We just scarf it up.

"First, these parents wouldn't let up about having a gluten-free classroom." Ma teaches the kindergartners at Kingston.

"No pizza for the kiddies, then." I shove another bite into my mouth.

"I mean, it's their choice, that's fine. I can keep gluten-free snacks around, but I can't impose them on the whole class."

"Separation of bread and state," Mee quips.

"And then"—Ma grabs another slice—"these parents tell me I should act more 'reasonably' because I've chosen an alternative lifestyle for myself." Ma wiggles her left ring finger, and Mee almost chokes on a piece of pineapple. (Hawaiian pizza is the king of pizzas.)

"Fuck 'em," I say. It's my mantra.

"Language!" Ma still manages to smile.

"What's wrong in the shop? People demanding gluten-free acupuncture?" I ask Mee.

"No, it's all this paperwork. I'm drowning in it."

"Paperwork for what?" Ma asks, wiping some grease from her cheek.

"Oh, . . . um . . . it's for this thing, for the shop. Trying to . . . ah . . . do some renovations." The pizza acts as a conversational sedative, and we all calm down between bites of ham, pineapple, and heaps of delicious gluten.

("·_·)(·_·")(☉_☉)

YP waits for me at my locker before class this morning. She texted last night, asking how I was doing, but I couldn't come up with an answer. I just didn't know.

"OKOK?" she asks, picking up on the way I sign the phrase. I waggle my head noncommittally, not really sure if I am OKOK. I wave for her to walk with me to class. I don't actually need anything in my locker anyway.

"You think painting was really bad?" YP signs most of the words.

"You know it *wasn't bad*."

"So why you—" She looks over her shoulder and stops walking. Kyle Stokers walks by us, arm slinked around some girl, hand crammed into her butt pocket. *Gross.* They're laughing. Arm Candy's covering her mouth, so I can't see what she's saying. I have a feeling it's not anything nice, judging by the look on YP's face.

"Uch. Let's go." She loops her arm through mine and we start down the hall again. It's strange. I thought the sight of KFS and Co. would bring on YP's waterworks. But she looks pissed. And it looks good on her.

She speeds up, walking faster in order to overtake him. Once we do, she turns to me and signs while walking.

"D O U C H E B A G."

"I couldn't agree more!" I sign.

"How sign 'asshole'?" she asks with a smile. I go right ahead and show her.

"Maybe YP can tutor you after—" Casey is droning on, as the three of us leave history class together.

"I'm not sure that's, like, the best idea." YP thankfully cuts her off.

"C'mon, Casey, I'm not that bad."

"What's going on?" Casey signs. A crowd blocks off the hall in front of the main office. YP and Casey both jump as someone slams the door to the office from the inside, keeping out the onlookers. Casey seems more curious than either of us and picks up the pace.

Shutting the door didn't do much to stop the crowd. The office is lined with windows facing the hallway. YP and Casey try to pick up on the students' whispers, but I'm still in the dark. Instead of looking into the office, I scan people's faces. Lots of concerned brows, some slack-jawed staring. Everyone seems to be asking the same thing: *Who?*

YP is the first of us to get a glimpse inside the office and makes a quick 180 to face me.

"Go. Class. Now," she signs, and runs off without another word. Casey and I elbow our way to the window just in time to see a fully uniformed police officer sternly shut the blinds.

~(₀☉_ʊ@)>

Everyone in Room 105 sits quietly, waiting for Mr. Katz to show up. Casey asked, but none of the students know where he is.

"What happened? Anyone know?" She's asking about the cop. *No one's going to talk to you, Casey. No one's going to spill it to a teacher.*

"I heard————graffiti." Freckles proves me wrong.

"Where, here at school?" Casey asks, eyes bugging out behind her glasses.

"Nah,——-——think——kid here did it," Black Shirt adds. He mumbles, his face is deadpan, I can't read it. I wave to Casey and ask her to start doing her job so I don't have to lip-read. She blushes and quickly starts interpreting for Freckles.

"That's so stupid. No one here is *that* good. Have you seen it?" I try to take her comment as a compliment, but she's so snotty about it, I can't tell if she's being sarcastic.

"Yeah," Black Shirt answers, "that skeleton is sick!"

The skeleton! What about the rest of it?! My ears burn hot again. All of our sketchbooks are ready, but there's nothing to draw. If the cops are here about the overpass, I doubt we're going to continue on with the street-art unit. *I can only hope.* The door swings open and Mr. Katz scrambles in, his hair falling wildly across his eyes.

"So sorry, class! Let's talk." He pulls a stool over to his

podium and takes a seat. Everyone in the class watches him expectantly. He taps his foot and opens his mouth, but says nothing. He has a few frustrated false starts before he finally begins.

"Who can . . . ah . . . tell me the difference between graffiti and vandalism?" I'm not going to be the first with my hand up.

"Is there a difference?" This question gets more responses. Everyone nodding, saying yes, there is a difference.

"So, what is it?"

"It's when you spray-paint something that's public property," the toy to my left answers.

"Is that vandalism or graffiti?" Katz raises his eyebrows.

"Oh, um . . ." She doesn't know.

"Graffiti elevates," I sign. Casey interprets, and all eyes are on me. *Shit*.

"Meaning?" Katz asks.

"I guess I'm saying that vandalism doesn't add anything to the world. It's all bravado."

"You don't think there's ego in street art?"

"That's not what I mean." I'm having a conversation. With a teacher. In a mainstream class. No one is laughing. My pits start to prickle with sweat. "Street art—graffiti—adds something to the world, something that makes you think, that makes you stop and notice something you might not have noticed before. Vandals tag for the sake of putting their name on a wall. Their intentions are crappy." Casey even says the word *crappy* verbatim. I can tell by the expression on Black Shirt's face.

"Do you think street art should be legal?" Katz breaks eye contact, directing the question at the whole class.

156

"Sure, if you get permission," Freckles chimes in.

"Yeah, there should be some sort of system in place," Black Shirt says. Funny that our token teen anarchist is calling for a system.

"Why?" I ask him. He hesitates, looking back and forth between me and Casey. He addresses her instead of me.

"The art can be in, like, specific places. Not randomly in your face or wherever."

"But there are billboards and advertisements everywhere in my face. No one asked for *my* permission." He looks confused. I press on.

"It's corporate vandalism, if you ask me. If they get to do it, why can't—" *Shit shit shit shit shit shit.* "Why can't . . . um . . . artists do it?"

The blinds are still drawn when YP and I pass by the main office again. I'm starting to realize what a problem my custom-painted car might be. Walking through the parking lot, I remember painting Lee. How hot it was, Jordyn hanging out in her two-piece, winking at the guys who walked by as I worked. When I finished, I knew. I knew there was no going back. I had found my place. This was my art.

YP: Youll raise red flags if you paint over it.

JULIA: You think?

YP: People will wonder why

JULIA: True

YP gets in shotgun. Her dad baked up a new pie recipe, and I begged to be a taste tester. She wants to talk to me about my next move, but it feels weird, talking about something that used to belong to me, and me alone.

YP: No talking plans round my dad okok?

JULIA: ofc.

She opens the front door to her house, and again the smell is heavenly. This time it's toffee, butter, something bitter. I love my parents, I really do. But this house makes me dream of what it would be like if Ma could bake something that doesn't come out of a tube.

"Julia!" I can feel her dad's deep voice in the air. I wave hi.

"I——good news!" he exclaims, pulling down plates. "Diane——-—-you can do Cheer tryouts——-—-problem." A slice of pecan pie lands heavily in front of YP.

"You did what?!" YP's hands fly into the air. She crosses the kitchen, shouting and gesturing, facing away. I can only see the hurt look in her dad's eyes as she stomps off to her room.

"Sorry,—-————," he mumbles to the ground before excusing himself. I'm sure the last thing YP wants right now is pie, but I bring two slices on my search for her bedroom. I follow her upstairs.

I can feel the floor vibrating as I get closer to her door; she's blasting some sort of music. Her door wrapped in that "POLICE LINE DO NOT CROSS" tape. I don't bother knocking. Police lines never stopped me before.

WHAT I EXPECTED YP'S ROOM TO LOOK LIKE:

Pink. Pink everywhere. Posters of dazzling blond pop sing-ers. Pom-poms hanging from the footpost of a white bed with swirling ironwork, adorned by frilly pillows and a marshmal-lowy down duvet. A little vanity table cluttered with makeup and earrings dangling from a stand. Topped off with a layer of stuffed animals as far as the eye can see.

WHAT YP'S ROOM LOOKS LIKE:

White. White everywhere. The walls are white, the bed is white, her curtains are white. She doesn't have a single poster, of a pop singer or otherwise. The only picture hanging on her wall is the one I drew of her the other day. Not even a family photo sitting on her white dresser. Even the speakers she's blasting music from are white. The only bit of color is that yellow tape on her door. And her, sitting on the edge of her bed, chewing her fingernail.

"What are you doing?" she asks without fingerspelling.
   "Bringing you pie?"
   "No, what you going do? What next?"
   "What was that all—" She cuts me off, waving the situa-tion out of the air.
   "Not matters, we have work to do," she tells me.
   "We?"
   "You——think I'm letting you——-next—-alone,— you?"

159

GRAFF OATH
FUCKING BINDING AND NON-NEGOTIABLE

I HEREBY PROMISE TO KEEP MY LIPS LOCKED. THIS MEANS:

> NO TELLING KIDS AT SCHOOL
>
> NO TWEETING
>
> NO FB
>
> NO INSTAGRAM
>
> NO BRAGGING
>
> NO PARENTS
>
> NO COPS

IF SOMETHING GOES DOWN I WILL RUN AS FAST AS I CAN TO THE MEETUP SPOT. I WILL NOT RUN TO THE SPOT:

> IF THE COPS ARE TAILING ME
>
> IF SOMEONE IS WATCHING ME

IF THE RUNNING DOESN'T WORK AND I GET CAUGHT:

> I GOT MY LIPS LOCKED UP. NO NAMES
>
> MY MOUTH STAYS CLOSED
>
> NO NAMES

COPS CAN'T CHARGE YOU WITH ANYTHING UNLESS THEY CATCH YOU IN THE ACT. ADMIT NOTHING.

IF I GET CAUGHT I REALIZE THAT IT'S PART OF THE GAME, AND I WILL TRY NOT TO TAKE IT OUT ON JULIA.

JULIA SWEARS TO DO EVERYTHING IN HER POWER TO MAKE SURE WE GET IN AND OUT SAFE, AND HOME IN TIME FOR PIE.

SIGNED

_____

She signs the paper without hesitation, not a question about one single bullet point. She doesn't make a fuss about what could happen if she gets caught. That's how I know she's really up for it. We burn it in her fireplace before clinking mugs of cocoa that her dad made by way of apology.

I feel better. Coming clean to YP about my whole deal means I don't always have to have my guard up. I know I should be more careful, but right now it feels like all my bases are covered.

Making my next move seems slightly less terrifying, knowing at least I have someone to keep my 6. Someone I can *actually* trust. Now all I need is more paint. And, you know, a game plan.

(; ☉_☉)

I drive right past the big blue whale-shaped school the next morning, checking up on the underpass. I wonder if the vandal squad has painted over it yet. Heh, the vandal squad. I wonder if they even *have* a vandal squad in the suburbs. Hard to believe they would need one, before now.

The cops aren't there this morning, but someone else is. I slow down a bit. Someone is taking pictures of it, with an old-school Polaroid camera, of all things. The photographer turns to leave the tunnel right as I drive past. Four big brown eyes lock onto each other for what seems like the longest second of my life. I blink and I'm under the sky again, leaving Mr. Katz, pockets full of pictures, dumbfounded in the tunnel.

눈_눈

Static. That's all my brain is capable of processing right now. After seeing Katz in the wild, I let my body switch to autopilot, and here I am in history class, unable to think about anything. My brain buzzes with fuzzy, scrambled images. Every thought I have is on some sort of weird delay, like when pixels on TV can't keep up with the video feed. Broken. *My brain is broken.*

Buzz through history, buzz through the halls, buzz through getting changed for gym. YP must know something is up; she's keeping her distance today. I can feel her watching me. *Do I tell her?* My brain won't allow me to think about what I saw for too long, yet it seems like it's the only thing I can think about. It makes so much sense, and no sense at all. My brain is pins and needles.

I've almost made it to winter break. One more day of classes until we are off for the holidays, and I'm spending it in a haze. Ms. Ricker has decided that our last gym class should be something "fun." She hands each of us a little device from a plastic basket. It looks like a cheap digital watch.

"Everyone clip the———-————-your————-okay?" she bellows, holding up one of the devices and clipping it to her shorts. I follow along, still on autopilot.

"We'll have a contest!————-————-most steps wins! Start running ------- go!" I was too busy staring at the ceiling to notice when she announced for us to start, and YP tugs me along on her second lap of the gym.

The little display counts up by one with every step I take. I like watching how fast the numbers climb. Ten, twenty-two, thirty. I jog around the gym with everyone else, letting the static wash over my thoughts until there's nothing but the numbers and the pounding of my heart.

YP is fast, much faster than me. I should be keeping in shape; I should be as fast as she is. How am I supposed to out-run the law at this pace? Maybe I should buy a bike. She laps me again, determined. She doesn't look down at her screen, she only looks ahead, staring at some imaginary finish line.

Kyle Fucking Stokers runs up beside her and says something that only makes her run even harder. He stops running altogether. I pass him and smirk over my shoulder. *Ha! Yeah, that's right, leave her alone.* The look he shoots back at me is almost enough to trip me and cause a six-kid pileup.

I'm excellent at reading facial expressions; they're an important part of my language. YP only signs with her hands. She doesn't have a grasp on her face yet. I understand her without expressions to read, but it's like she's speaking with an accent. It's like watching someone dance but they don't move their arms. Awkward.

KFS's expression isn't one I've seen before. It's not pity, not the look you'd give to a wounded animal, a look I'm used to getting daily. It's an odd mixture of pure hatred and hopelessness. It asks: *What are you trying to do?* What *am* I trying to do? Why is *he* asking me?

. . .

"What's up with you today?" YP signs back in the locker room. She's flushed after winning the mini-competition.

"I'm worried, I guess." I pull my black sweater over my vintage, thrift-shop Keith Haring tee.

"About—" She looks over her shoulder, forgetting no one else in here can understand us. "About W A T E R T O W E R?"

"DUH," I sign, and stick out my tongue.

"I have plan. Urban Café Sunday?"

"Not now?"

"No, no, no, I have-——-——- I need to get————-." YP opens her prize for winning, a chocolate protein bar, with her teeth and takes an enormous bite. She smiles at me, mouth full, on her way out of the locker room.

Mr. Katz doesn't show up for his class.

(￣~￣)

On my way to work, my focus sharpens. Everything that was covered in static becomes clearer the farther I drive from school. The street-art unit, the paint in the supply cabinet. He's seen my car, he's heard the song. He knows it's me, and I *know* it's him.

Taking Polaroids, showing up late, not showing up at all. He's revealing his hand. And after this morning, it might as well be painted red. Maybe that's why he didn't come to class—he couldn't face the fact that his rival is onto him.

Part of me wants to text YP right now, tell her what was really going on this morning. I was fine blowing up Donovan's spot when I thought it was him. But Katz? He could get in real trouble. I guess we both could. So I'll keep his secret as long as he keeps mine.

I want to take it as a compliment, that a teacher I look up to decided my art was worthy of the conversation, but I can't get my gut to agree with my brain. Just because he's a teacher doesn't make him better, doesn't give him the right to my art, my walls. He can't insert himself into my conversations like that. I didn't give him permission. Permission. *Fuck*. That whole street-art talk, all that crap about permission. Was he trying to absolve himself?

See, Julia? Katz asks in my head. *No one needs anyone's*

permission, you said so yourself. Your art's open season. Let me show you how it's done.

I change into my fry-girl uniform and lock away all my stuff. I haven't talked to Jordyn since that night in my car, so when she sashays into the locker room and sees me standing there, she does a little double-take.

"Coming or going?" she asks.

"Coming."

"So, you *are* back at it. Why didn't you tell me?"

"Are *you really* asking *me* that?"

"But you told that girl." I don't respond. She won't understand, I've been anti-hearie, anti-implant, anti-friends, anti-everything for so long, so how do I explain that this random, bubbly cheerleader happens to *get* me? I hardly understand it myself.

"She's fat. And weird." Jordyn wiggles her fingers under her nose, grimacing.

"Shut the fuck up. You don't know her."

"There's something not right there."

"I'm done talking to you."

"She's hiding something." She puts her visor on and leaves without letting me have my say.

I know YP. We've talked more than enough for me to piece it together. The pies, the weight, the cheerleaders, Kyle. It's not exactly an uncommon story. She hasn't explicitly said what happened, but she doesn't need to. The fact that Jordyn spent all of an hour with YP and feels entitled to judge her reminds me exactly why I didn't tell her that I'm "back at it." Why I'm never telling her anything again.

. . .

When I get to my station I see that Donovan is planted in the drive-thru. Great, another third-wheel shift. I throw down my first batch of fries and hope the steam is so hot I evaporate with it. Jordyn is still pretty protective of him, too, winking and blowing kisses whenever she catches his eye. Making a big show of their relationship, just in case I forget. He looks worn out, exasperated. It's a familiar expression. I've seen it on Jordyn's face dozens of times. Once again I'm thankful for my deafness. It's much easier to ignore Jordyn's giggling face than the actual giggles.

The oil is sparkling, rolling, bubbling, beautiful, yellow. That color would look sweet on the water tower, if I could only find a way to get up there. I'm actually excited that YP has thought of something. I expected to be put out, but I've never seen her so revved up before. Never seen her shove food into her mouth with a smile. Maybe she'll feel better soon, cry less. Learn to not give a fuck. Like me.

Golden, foamy, deep-fried letters standing out against the mint green of the water tower. A grease stain you can't wash out. I'm HERE, Katz. *Now what?*

My socks are soaked through with sweat when I peel them off after my shift. Donovan comes into the locker room and flicks the lights to get my attention. He has it. He leans against the door, nervous. His hands tremble as he reaches into his pocket and waves for me to come over. I pad over the cold tile floor in my bare feet.

I arch my eyebrows, miming, *Yes?*

"Here." He pulls out a little package wrapped in silver paper, nearly drops it on the ground before putting it in my hand.

"Merry Christmas," he mumbles.

"It's not—"

"Open it," he demands, still barricading the locker-room door with his back. I peel the tape off. It still has the little plaid Scotch tape–header piece on it. The small present is heavy, and wrapped without a box.

"Hurry up!" he motions, paddling his hand in a circle. I slide the contents into my hand.

Magnets. It's a column of plain, black, round magnets. I look up at him and he's giving me his best Donovan drive-thru megawatt smile.

"Thanks?" is all I can sign.

"—-for——paint, you liar."

"What?"

"You know," he signs haltingly, trying to remember the right hand shapes, "how I know about you?"

I shake my head. My face feels hotter than it gets over the fryer.

"——cans rattle," he says.

"No!" I cross my arms. He's wrong. He has to be. I always holster each one in a loop, to avoid that very thing.

"—-————-inside the can, you know,——you shake it?" Donovan mimes shaking a can.

Holy shit. I never . . .

He cracks up. I'm sure the look on my face is priceless.

"Put them on the bottom of the cans." He acts out the motion with an invisible can, when suddenly the door opens a crack, pushing him forward. He shoves me away and jolts to his locker before Jordyn tries to open the door again. The three of us change without so much as a sign.

(ФДФ) ✦

I wait until Jordyn and Donovan leave before pulling my black bag out from under my car seat. Damn, here I was dreaming up some masterpiece in yellow, and all I have is the near-empty Katz cans. Black, blue, and purple.

They're freezing from sitting in the car; can't be good for the paint. I shake up the purple can. I can barely feel the little ball sliding back and forth in there. It's that noisy? Noisy enough for him to hear it through my bag. *Shit*. I shake it up again, trying to feel the sound, putting it up to my cheek. It's barely there, and I might be imagining it. I've always seen *[keys jingle]*, but *[paint rattles]*? Never.

The magnets are nestled in my coat pocket back in their silver paper wrapping. If this had happened a few weeks ago, it would have made sense: another tipoff to the role I thought he was playing in our game. Now, I'm confused as hell. How would he even know about this little trick?

I can't help but think it's pretty cute. The silver paper, the tape. If Jordyn was jealous before, I can't imagine how she feels now. I wonder if he got *her* a Christmas gift. I'm supposed to be backing off. I already broke up with him in my head. It seems impossible to break it off with him now.

It's getting late. The magnets snap to the bottoms of the cans. I shake them one by one, hoping that's enough to guide the metal balls to the magnets. It's brilliant. Whatever sound they made before, they certainly won't make again. *Stupid sound.*

9(⊙‿⊙)6

Ma is asleep on the couch when I get home. I hate bringing my stash anywhere near the house, but I can't leave it in school unattended, especially with the cops snooping around. Mee waves from the top of the stairs.

"Come come come on!"

"OKOK." I kick off my shoes before joining her.

She leads me into my room and sits on my bed next to a yellow folder. She's practically bouncing with excitement.

"I got you a present!" she finally announces. *Two presents in a day?*

"For what?" I furrow my brow.

"Just, because." She can tell I don't buy it, so she continues. "Because you made it through the semester. I know it wasn't easy." My stomach churns. She has no idea. It wasn't easy, not because of classes, but because of stencils and rivals and stolen paint. And now she's rewarding me for—what? For going behind her back, after I promised them both it was over? I wish she would stop telling me how good I'm being.

"Here." She hands me the folder and claps her hands together. I don't want to open it. I don't deserve whatever it is.

"Go on," she urges.

I stick my fingers in the folder like I'm holding my place in a book. I should hand it back, tell her everything. My stupid hands work against me and open it anyway. Paperwork.

172

I flip through the sheets, all headed with the words *QUEENS COUNTY*. The more I read, the more excited Mee gets and the worse I feel. I can't believe she did this. She got me a wall. The biggest side of her acupuncture studio. A legal wall for me to paint on whenever I want. And what have I done? Lied to her. All damn year.

I'm going to throw up.

I tell Mee a thousand times how great it is, how happy I am, it's so perfect, thanks so much! I'm praying she can't tell as my stomach somersaults. I hug her out of my bedroom before heading to the only room in the house with a lock, and hurl up a small fry and Coke.

My forehead rests on the toilet seat. I'm not getting up until I'm sure I'm finished. I feel my phone buzz in my pocket; it's YP.

YP: omgcheck yr email.

I close out the message and open up my mail. She's sent me a link with no subject line or any other info. It leads to an article:

TEACHER TRYING TO SAVE STREET ART

In the small Long Island town of Greenlawn, one art teacher doesn't want to clean up his neighborhood's graffiti—he wants to preserve it. Andy Katz, 31, a teacher at Finley High School, has been in talks with City Council and the Greenlawn Police Department for the past week, defending the graffiti as works of art and attempting to bar the city's typical cleanup procedures.

The first recipient of Katz's preservationist attention was a mural on the back of a scoreboard at Tri-Village Field, depicting a whale and its skeleton. After meeting with Mr. Katz, the owner of the park, Cliff Ferguson, has decided to preserve the "art."

"I think it's interesting," Ferguson said about the mural. Because the graffiti was created on his property, if Ferguson chooses not to press charges, law enforcement must drop the incident.

A second work of graffiti that local police say was painted by the same individual appeared recently on the Spring Road underpass. It depicts a woman with seashells for eyes, similarly overlaid with a skeleton. It's been painted on public property managed by the Suffolk County Department of Public Works. Local government, however, is adhering to policy in responding to the incident.

"You vandalize city property, you're going to have a bad time," Watch Commander Cox quipped in a phone interview. He was also quick to dismiss the efforts of Mr. Katz to preserve these works. "I get it. Artists like to stick up for their own. But when it comes down to it, it's not real art, is it? It's the defacing of public property that costs the city money to clean up."

Besides presenting his impassioned view in a City Council public hearing last Thursday, Katz has filed a petition with Suffolk County to prevent cleanup of the Spring Road mural. He is also "investigating [his] options" for obtaining an injunction against the DPW. According to Katz, the fight is not over. Whether it is an eyesore or an artwork, at this moment, the Spring Road mural is still there.

I hurl one more time for good measure.

. . .

Underneath my quilt, the light shines through the squares like stained glass. I'm supposed to want this. Public reaction, someone saying they want to actually preserve a piece. This should be the happiest night of my life.

What an ego, that Katz. Let your graff go. Don't babysit your writing, don't take pictures, don't talk to the fucking press! Oh, and how about, don't bring your girlfriend into it? And while I'm at it, don't date your student's interpreter! You're a great artist, but your toy is showing.

City property. This is the problem with wars. Considering the article and the cops, I wouldn't be caught dead bombing public property twice in a row. Hit up the side of a shop or something.

It's too hot. I can't breathe. It stinks under here. I need a shower. I need a plan.

I need YP.

JULIA: Come over?

The hall lights flash off and on; she's here. I step into my slippers and go downstairs. Mee is already standing in the doorway, YP slowly signing introductions. Mee asks YP to take off her shoes. I must have looked exactly like that when her dad answered the door for me. Scared out of my mind, totally out of my element. Mee turns around to get my attention but I'm already standing behind her.

"You didn't tell me you made a new friend!" Mee smiles uncontrollably. YP and I smile, too.

"It's late; is everything okay?" she asks, addressing both of us. YP picks up on the *okay* bit and signs that she's fine.

"We're having a sleepover," I explain as I pull YP past Mee and up to my room. My mom stomps her foot when we reach the top of the stairs.

"Love you."

"Your mom deaf, too?" YP sits down on the floor in front of my bed.

"Yep. Both of them are," I sign.

"Wait, both? Both what?"

"Both moms."

"And they are deaf, and you are deaf?"

I nod.

"How?"

This is the problem with me and YP. It's nothing I wouldn't tell her—I mean, she already knows the real secret stuff. I want to be able to tell her, to talk to her like we both speak the same language, not to have to reach for a phone or paper. Every big conversation has to be a struggle.

She waves me back from space.

"Sorry," I sign. "It's C O M P L I C A T E D."

"Here." She grabs my laptop off of the bed. I roll my eyes. Always with the typing.

"Don't be stupid." She hits her forehead, her fingers in a V shape. Pants opens up the laptop on the floor and lies down in front of it. She waves me down to join her. I open up a Word file and let my fingers fly, English grammar be damned. YP won't care.

My moms wanted baby right? So they decided they
would get a donor and have one that way. Ma was

176

working for tenure so Mee say that she will have the baby. So they had this friend who's Deaf give them . . . the stuff right? And blah blah I was born.

SO like, if you're both deaf you'll have a deaf baby?

No, its a chance. They not know for sure that I would be Deaf. They say even if i was hearing they wouldnt care, they just wanted a baby. But I turned out to be Deaf.

Are you mad?

for what?

Maybe you wouldn't be deaf if . . .

I like being Deaf.

Oh.

Im big D deaf btw.

What?

use the big D Deaf not little d deaf.

Theres a difference?

yeah bc being Deaf is part of who i am. Im proud of it, I have a community. Im part of it.

It's so hard to explain, I don't know how to make YP understand the ins and outs of Deaf culture in a way that would
make sense to her, or any hearing person. Ma is better at this
stuff. The whole "it's not hearing-loss, it's Deaf-gain" thing.
I'm not a spokesperson for us, but I do love our community.
I know how to explain it in sign, but not so well in English.

Thats really cool!!! I had no idea :)

you seem like youre feeling happier.

I feel like . . . like I'm me again. But better.

even without cheerleading or whatever?

Cheer wasn't me.

(̄~ ̄)

SERIOUSLY!!! I liked it because it meant I had friends.

but they're so mean!

I know, but I didn't care! I didn't have to be alone.

Alone not so bad.

It gets old.

so you're done with them? all the cheer girls??

Yes. I feel like, I'm back . . . I'm here.

I pick at the carpet. I think YP senses something is off. Her eyes dart around my room like she's looking for something new to talk about. I rip out a thread when she finds the Jordyn box.

"Ooh, ex-boyfriend stuff?" she signs, and shakes the box like a kid with a present.

"Ex-friend stuff." I snatch the box away from her.

"——-I see?" YP scoots next to me. We lean against the edge of my bed.

"Sure, I guess." I give the box back to her and let her open it. As soon as she does I can't help but laugh. It's unexpected and I'm caught off guard, but it all seems so silly now. I was moping over what, a selfie stick?

"Oh, it's just stuff." YP reads my mind again. "I thought——-be more, I don't know." We lay it all out on the floor and finally have a real sense of what my friendship with Jordyn was about. Convenience. Outcasts banding together so we wouldn't be so alone. And for a while that worked, but we're just too different. And not in that good, "opposites attract" way. Now I see that she sort of glommed on because I didn't judge or shame her. I'm sure that was comforting for her, and I don't think she's done anything to be ashamed of, but what exactly did she add to my life? A shoe box full of random stuff. It's hard to believe I was so heartbroken over it.

"I'm happy I met you," I sign to YP, and she practically glows.

"Same." She uses the right sign, sliding her hand in the Y shape back and forth between us. "Oh, I———forgot! Check———out!" YP stands up and unzips her quilted duffel bag and pulls out two yellow vests. On the backs, the words *SUFFOLK COUNTY* are stenciled in black.

"I have jumpsuits, too!" She reveals a pant leg from the bag.

"Isn't this going to make us, you know, stand out?" I pulse my fingers like flashing lights.

"Nuh-uh." She shakes her head, her bangs swoosh around. "————-look like the city hired——fix it."

"That's brilliant!" I sign, and flop onto the bed. "But—" I sign to the ceiling. She's really thought this through; I'm seriously impressed. The effort that went into the outfits . . .

"What——?" She flops down next to me.

"I don't know if I can do it."

Someone is shaking me along with my alarm. I open my eyes and a wide-eyed YP points to the bed over and over again.

"Where is it?!" She blushes and covers her mouth, waiting for my response.

"What? Where's what?" I sign.

"Your . . . *you know.*" She shakes her fingers, then starts spelling, "V I B R A–"

"No!" I cut her off, pinching my fingers. "Are you crazy?"

"It must've switched on—————-," she says, lifting a corner of my quilt.

"I don't have a—" *Oh.* I'm finally awake enough to realize what's going on. I slap the button on my alarm clock and the bed stops vibrating. My bed alarm is intense. I had to get one called the Ultra Shaker. It was the only alarm annoying enough to actually get me out of bed.

"My alarm," I tell her. She doesn't catch the sign, so I spell it out.

"Jeez,——- I thought————————an earthquake or —
————-. Then I thought . . . um . . . well. Yeah."

She *is* crazy. I comb out my hair with my fingers before tucking it under my beanie.

"So? You ready?" She picks up the duffel bag.

"I told you, I don't think I'm ready. I don't think I can—"

"Uch, don't be all like that. Get dressed; we're going out." She skips into the hall with her toothbrush.

Since when is she in charge? I know I *can* do it; that's not the point. This whole mess hasn't given me a second to think. They tag back too fast. Stealing paint, hitting city property, and telling people—it doesn't feel right. I like to plan, take my time. Be thoughtful, not reckless. It feels messy. YP doesn't care though, she wants me to see it through. I really don't know why she cares so much. Not just about this, about everything.

$$(\cdot \_ \cdot ")/\backslash(\cdot \_ \cdot ")$$

"**W**here are we going?" I sign with one hand and swipe my MetroCard with the other.

"I read————-——place on Google." I want to tell her you don't read about anything on Google itself, but whatever.

It's freezing this afternoon up on the elevated platform for the 7 train. It hasn't snowed in a few days, but gray drifts clump to the bases of trash cans and benches. It's disgusting. The snow over by Finley stays beautiful and clean for weeks. Not this nasty, gritty sludge that coats the entire borough of Queens.

"You drive long to go F I N L E Y every day, huh?" YP signs.

"I guess. Didn't have a choice."

"You go to the city a lot?" she asks.

I want to lie and say, "Of course, I'm always there. Definitely not spending all my free time at McDonald's and in my basement." The train pulls up and spares me from answering her. YP sits on her knees facing the window, her finger running across someone's scratch tag.

"You like?" she asks.

"No." I shake my head, and sit forward.

"Y?" she signs, using shorthand of her own invention. Sort of like texting, she'll sign only one letter instead of the word. It's really wrong, but it's pretty cute.

"Trashy. Ugly. Doesn't *mean* anything," I tell her, and she smiles.

"Come on, it's our stop." YP walks to the door before the train stops, like a true New Yorker.

"Already?" I stand up to follow her, and as soon as I glance out the windows, I know where we're going.

It's 5 Pointz. The Institute of Higher Burnin'. Anyone who's ever dreamed of bombing a wall in New York knows about 5 Pointz, the giant yellow graffiti Mecca. I've never done any writing on those sacred walls. My work is better than ever, but I know I have a ways to go before I can throw up anything worthy there.

We walk up Jackson Avenue, the building towering over us, colors spilling down every surface. Painted, bombed, muraled, tagged, and painted over and over again. Paradise.

"I lied." YP stops walking and looks down at her feet. "I not Google it."

"So?"

"Mr. Katz took a few of us here last year."

"You went?" I ask. She nods yes, frowning. "I don't understand."

She takes out her phone and starts texting, even though we've been doing great without it today.

YP: Dont be mad.

JULIA: ok what

YP: He took some kids from his class

JULIA: ok so and?

YP: I was in his class.

JULIA: art class?

YP: yea.

JULIA: you do art?

YP: used to. for fun or whatever.

JULIA: why you think I'm mad?

YP: It's your thing.

JULIA: I dont own all art. katz class is fun.

YP: I know.

JULIA: too bad we not in class together.

YP: yeah. anyway. I thought you should see this
place. get inspired

JULIA: it might be working ;)

186

YP puts her phone away and points to a chain-link fence blocking the entrance to the building. We both grip the fence, our fingers curling around the links, and read the official sign posted in front of us.

NO TRESPASSING:
VIOLATORS WILL BE PROSECUTED

COMING SOON:
THE BALLSTON
LUXURY LIVING IN THE HEART OF QUEENS.

"No way," YP looks back up at the building. "They can't do that, can they?"

"Fuck no, they can't."

We run along the fence looking for a break in the chain link, anywhere we can squeeze through. Turning the first corner, we see the fence is secure. It extends around the entire perimeter, down to the ground and at least six feet up, and is topped with barbed wire. I slow down and walk along it, my fingers brushing the links.

"Maybe————keep———, like artsy condos?" YP suggests, and I give her the most skeptical face I can muster.

The fence rattles against my hand. We both look down the length of it. There's a man trying to get over the barbed wire from inside the fence. He's put his black blazer over the barbs to protect his hands, but his tie snags on the way down. He wildly swipes at his caught tie with one hand, hanging on with the other. I grab YP's arm as we both run to meet him. I throw her my bag and climb up alongside the man.

"Go,—-, get—-—-ere!" He swats at me, trying to keep me from helping him.

"Stop struggling!" I use my voice, and he looks at me, startled. I reach up and pull his suit jacket from the barbs. It comes free cleanly and I toss it down to YP. I climb a little higher to get within reach of his tie. I think he starts talking again, but I don't look back at him. My gaze is fixed in front of me—past the tie, past the fence, to the wall straight ahead.

It's the most beautiful throwie I've ever seen. A spray can turns into a tower on fire that turns into a blossoming tree. Little pink flowers bloom from charcoal branches.

YP shakes the fence, snapping me back to reality. She signs for me to hurry up and I focus on the stranger's tie, the end of which is splattered with droplets of pink paint. As soon as I unhook him, he jumps down to the pavement and starts running. YP takes off after him, and I follow behind.

The dude is fast, but YP might be faster, even while carrying his jacket and both of our bags. She's gaining on him, and I'm struggling to keep up. *Run faster!* My Doc Martens dig into my ankles and my run turns into more of a skip, which turns into an all-out *splat* as I turn the corner. *Damn ice.*

I can't see YP or the Suit anymore, but she ditched my bag in the alley. I guess it was weighing her down? The alley branches off onto at least three streets, all bustling with people. I try to read expressions, see if anyone looks shocked or is watching the runners, but everyone is preoccupied with their phones, or work, or whatever.

I'm not rolling the dice on this one. The odds are stacked against me. YP will head back to 5 Pointz eventually, right? That's what I would do, I wouldn't just abandon her. My socks have slipped down from my ankles and only cover my toes; I unlace the boots and hike them up into place before heading back the way I came.

No point in running. I take my time. I can't get the image of the stranger in the suit out of my head. The look on his face . . . He was so *angry*. I was only trying to help. His dark skin and wild hair, the crinkles around his eyes. Not really old, but older than I would have pegged a bomber brave enough to jump barbed wire, and in the middle of the day. Who does that?

I know who. I just can't believe it.

What's he doing in Queens? If that's him, everyone's got it wrong. I always held out hope that Banksy was a woman. But I'll take a dude with an Afro in a business suit over an old pasty guy any day. No one would believe me! I barely believe it myself. In fact, I wouldn't at all if I hadn't seen his graffiti. There's imitators of his work, sure, but there's no faking his style.

I check my phone. No texts from Pants, no missed calls. I go to open my mail and there's a tap on my shoulder. I jolt and the phone slides from my fingers and smashes into the ground.

"Fuck!" I yell, pick up my phone, and turn around.

on't. Don't move. Can you move? Can you breathe? What are you doing? Say something! Hello? Say something! Lift your hands and tell him you know. Don't just stand there. Are you dreaming? There he is, right there. So close you could . . . what? Touch him? *Do not touch him.* When did the sky get so pink? How long have you been standing there? Say something! He smells like aerosol and dynamite. His eyes are black; the grin he cracks is even blacker, devilish and dark.

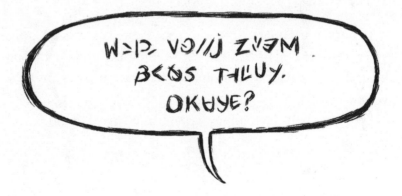

What? What? What? I can't understand him, it's like he's speaking another language. The mouth shapes aren't making sense. He's talking too fast. My stomach turns over, I'm missing it. *He's talking to me and I'm missing it.*

He smiles again and leans in. He places a hand on my

shoulder and whispers in my ear. I can feel the hum of his voice, his warm breath snakes in and tickles a spot in me I didn't know was there. He steps back and all I can do is shake my head. I don't break eye contact. YP turns a corner, a block behind him, and stops in her tracks.

The Suit's smile vanishes. He points to his ear and raises one perfect eyebrow. I nod my head, raise my arms. *Oh, fucking well.* He reaches out and puts his thumb in the dimple on my chin. Then, he stands straight up and he signs:

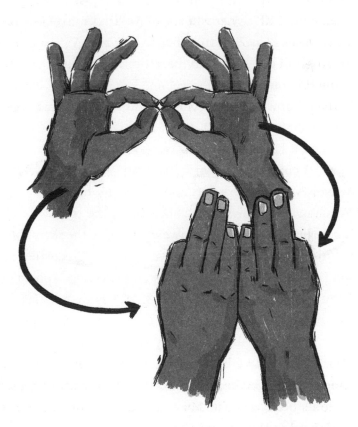

That's it. He straightens his tie and walks off.

. . .

"What———say?!" YP huffs, on our way back to the 7 train.

"I don't know," I sign. "I couldn't understand him." She looks disappointed. She has only her bag now; she must've ditched his coat in the chase. "It's not my fault! He was talking too fast or something."

"He had an A C C E N T," she clarifies, and bites one of her polished pink nails.

"Shit."

"Yeah. Shit," YP signs, and starts walking in front of me.

"You're mad at me?!" I turn her to face me.

"You let him go!" she yells, hands in her pockets.

"What do you care?"

"You not know, who that?!" Her signs are sharp and angry.

"Yes!" I shake my fist. "I didn't *want* to let him—"

"You could have stopped—"

"Wait." I cut her off. "You *know* him?" I see her searching for the words, her fingers curl and uncurl by her sides.

"Whole world knows him." She boards the train.

I ignore her by sketching a few more signs in the sketchbook I'm making for Katz. But somewhere between Bliss Street and Jackson Heights we both calm down and exchange apologies.

"Why paint there now?" she asks. "It's not gonna last."

"Maybe it will. Maybe someone will want to save it."

"Like Mr. Katz?" She elbows my side and giggles.

"*He's* trying to save his own ass. Banksy wants to save us all." We get off the train and wander back to where I parked Lee. YP puts her bag in the backseat next to mine before sitting backward in the passenger seat.

"What you mean, save ass?" YP asks, leaning against the glove box. When we sit like this, I don't have to keep looking over while I drive.

"You mean with Katz?" I sign one-handed. "He's trying to save his own graff. It's so . . ." I bring my hands up to my head and pull them away. "Big-headed, you know?"

"He's saving *your* work," she says.

"And *his*!"

"You mean, you think?"

"Totally."

"Wow!" She shakes her hand. "That's pretty cool, right?" Her signs keep getting better. If I drove her somewhere a month ago, we'd look out the window and not say a word. Now we're hanging out on the weekends and chasing down Banksy.

"Not really," I tell her. "He should do his own work, he doesn't have to school me on the street."

"But and . . . um . . . don't take————-wrong way— don't you think it looks good?"

"Psh! Yeah. I do. That's the problem. He isn't some sort of co-conspirator." (I spell it out for her.) "He's competition."

"But why?" She deflates. She always wants to be friends with everyone. Even if it means being sick to keep them. Not everyone has to be your friend, some people are just enemies. I sigh, and put both hands on the wheel. How do I explain the rules of a game that has no rules? He could have asked first, could have let me know some other way. He didn't have to goad me on with personal Post-its and one-ups. He obviously knows it's me and doesn't care. *It's insulting.*

"I don't know," I tell her as we drive up to her house. She

reaches over the seat and grabs her stuff before getting out of the car.

"When?" she signs through the window.

"When I get paint."

"Paint?" she signs, shocked. "No no no, W H E A T P A S T E."

ಠ_ಠ

Wheatpaste has always seemed like cheating to me. It takes a lot of the fun out of writing, since there's so much less risk involved. Yeah, it's still putting art up on a wall for the world to see, but it's too easy.

All I would have to do is mix up some flour and water, easy enough to sneak past my parents, and I'd have some pretty impenetrable glue. I could spend hours on the art itself, spread out on papers across the basement floor, and just tell my folks it's for class. Pack it up if they do catch on, but I could always pull it out and work on it some more. Then, I'd take the papers, and the glue, and a big-ass brush down to Greenlawn. It'd be up on that water tower in what—a minute?

Shit. She's right. Again. Wheatpaste might seem like cheating under normal circumstances, but these circumstances are far from normal. Everything else is a huge risk, so why not make it easier on myself? I don't even have to get my hands on spray paint. I can do it all with markers.

The light above my workstation blinks and I shake the excess oil off of the finished fries. School's out, but Mickey D's never closes. Come on down and get some fries at 4:30 a.m. You can be sure someone will be here to shake, salt, and sack 'em up for you.

Thankfully, I never have to work those weird night-owl shifts. It's only 10:00 p.m., and I'll be out soon enough. I put in the next frozen batch and the oil bubbles up as they're submerged. Maybe this isn't what I want to say on my tower piece. I thought I wanted to write about this place, this bit of my life. But that was before. Before 5 Pointz, before the barbed wire, before Banksy. Now I'm in the after.

Two days A.B. and fryer oil–styled letters leave a bitter aftertaste in my mouth. It's not big enough. It has to be huge. Enormous. Fat. Grande. Plus-sized. Supersized. The lights blink again, and I shuffle more fries into their boxes and bags.

Donovan turns around and wipes his forehead with his arm, exhaling deeply. I expect him to wink and flash one of his smiles, but instead, he walks to the locker room without a glance in my direction. Any swag he ever had has been sapped away. It wasn't even a busy shift. Who broke his crayons? Jordyn isn't on the schedule today, so neither of us has to work under a microscope. It's refreshing. I don't need any more lectures from her about my choice of boys or friends or "pastimes." I let him sulk in the drive-thru and go back to my fries.

It's nice having a monotonous job on days when my brain is full. I could handle the station one-handed—heck, one-legged. Sometimes I think my manager invented the position for me so he can say he hired a disabled person. Clearly he's obeying whatever laws he needs to obey. Invented position or not, I still get paid for doing hardly more than sweating ten gallons a shift. Not too bad.

Two days A.B. and I know it's time to aim higher, cut deeper. *Make a fucking statement.* I feel my phone buzz in my pocket. I want to check it, but I've been busted checking it before. I wonder how many warnings I get before they fire me over it. I check my 6 and it's clear. The place is dead; only one lonely old man sits in a booth toward the front. He comes in a lot. He likes to nibble at a no. 4 while people-watching for hours. I risk it and slide my cell out of my pocket just enough to read the text.

555-8920: Can we talk?

Should I know this number? I've never plugged it in. Then again, I don't really take the time to add contacts when I meet people. I have about six people on my phone. Before I can ask who it is, he texts again.

555-8920: Ill wait.

The last hour of my shift trudges on. The chick with the glasses clocks in, and there's no way I'm texting back with her around. Rumor has it she's a tattle, and she loves to stare whenever Jordyn and I sign. Tonight, she has nothing better to do than watch me like I'm some sort of unicorn, because we only get four more customers. I can't distract myself with my blinking alarm or bagging fries, because no one's buying.

My phone burns a hole in my pocket. I keep wrapping my fingers around it, running my fingertips along the cracks in the screen. I'll never have the cash to fix it. It's not on my priority list right now. I want him to text again. Gimme a little help here. I pace back and forth in front of my station, waiting for another message or customer or grease fire to break out, anything. Screw it. It's only five minutes early. I pull the baskets out of the oil and head through the kitchen. Glasses waves her arms at me.

"What?" I express with a sharp gesture rather than words. She sternly points to the clock, eyebrows arched so high they may fly off her head. I grandly present to her, with a sweep of my arm and bend of my knees, one empty chain restaurant. I wiggle my fingers as I wave good-bye.

Donovan sits hunched over on the bench in the locker room, head in his hands. I've never seen him like this, defeated. Did he not hear me come in? I stomp my foot and he jolts around to face me.

"You?" I hold up my phone.

"Me." He points to himself. I text him back.

JULIA: how you have my number?

555-8920: stole it

JULIA: whats wrong?

555-8920: wat u think?

JULIA: she break up with you?

555-8920: no

JULIA: then what?

555-8920: i need 2 break up w u

What is he talking about? I look up from my phone. He's facing the wall again. I wish he wouldn't; I need to see his face. Expressions don't come across in texts, though I suppose I can guess.

JULIA: (ಠ_ಠ)
we are not together.

555-8920: no shit

"So, what the fuck?" I stomp my foot again, and gesture sharply. He turns and scowls before going back to his phone.

555-8920: dont play stupid u know she doesnt
want us to talk.

JULIA: so? dont talk to me then.

555-8920: but wat if i want to talk 2 u

I don't want to blush, but it creeps over my cheeks anyway. Donovan notices and smiles, that stupid perfect smile, and I try my best not to melt away. I'm cold as ice, I don't care about him or the magnets or his perfect arm hairs.

JULIA: u want to talk break up with her.

555-8920: well thats no fun.

Gross. I brush past him to get to my locker. Get me out of here. I have bigger things to worry about. Jordyn's love life and Donovan's gross games do not register on the list. Donovan places a hand on my shoulder and turns me around to face him.

"I can't," he signs slowly. "I like you. And I know you like me."

"Not anymore."

(ʊ . ʊ)

Everyone in my dreams has telepathy. It's rare for anyone to sign or talk. We're all psychically linked. But tonight, there's no one to connect with. Someone must have poured sand in my boots because my feet are heavy; they drag along the pavement. Every step I take is more labored than the last. I have to go faster than this. Why are my shoes making me so slow?

I use my arms to lift my legs, step after step, pound after pound. I'm not getting any closer. *I have to go faster than this.* I should take the boots off. But I won't. I need them.

STOMP. STOMP. STOMP. The ground shakes. I look up. The water tower looms over my head, water dripping and spraying from the rivets. I need to go, I need to run. Why can't I run? I look down at my yellow shoes. *Just take them off, Julia!*

My feet start to fuse with the asphalt. Everything gets hot. Too hot. I can feel the water spraying my neck, soaking my hair. Where is everyone? Someone help me! I can't stay here. The heat rises up through my feet, past my ankles, burns my calves. It's unbearable. The supports start to buckle and shake.

"Fine!" I yell up to the tower. I have to take off my boots, but as soon as I touch the laces, everything flashes white. It's unbearable. I can't do it, I can't move, I can't take them

off. I'm on fire. I'm drowning. I'm burning. I need help. Someone . . .

STOMP. STOMP. STOMP.
STOMP. STOMP. STOMP.
STOMP. STOMP. STOMP.

My bed shakes me awake.

(#+_+)

Christmas comes and goes, and the few days after fly by. YP and I finally set a date: December 31, 11:59 p.m. Tonight we tag the water tower. My parents are going to their annual Deaf karaoke New Year's extravaganza, and with any luck, the cops will be overwhelmed with all sorts of non-graffiti-related shenanigans.

The basement is cold and I don't have to meet YP for at least an hour. I plug in my space heater and settle into my armchair. I flip open the Katz sketchbook and draw the signs for the words *queen* and *win,* even though I haven't actually won yet. I try to think of a few more words but they don't come. My pencil's ready, but my arm isn't. Maybe I don't want to draw more. Maybe, right now, nothing is better than something.

I miss being invisible and impossible to understand. Everyone is onto me, getting into my business. Donovan, Katz, Casey. Even Banksy signing at me. *Family?* Really? You don't know me. No one actually knows me. Except YP. She's allowed to stick around. Everyone else is a poser.

She's been texting me all day. Not saying anything important, but obviously very enthusiastic. I don't know why I'm not. Mee gave me some paint rollers for Christmas, and wants to know why she can't see the plans I've been working very hard on down in my lair. I don't know what to say to her anymore. Every word I sign is a lie, and it's exhausting.

The clock counts down to go time, and I throw in the towel with this whole sketching thing. It's obviously not coming to me tonight. This can't be what Katz wanted. He was probably trying to be playful, encouraging even. It's not like he made my art worse, not like he actually defaced it. What we make *is* bigger than both of us. But he took it too far. Expected too much of me. I wish I could talk to him.

I wear my Warhol flowers T-shirt underneath the coveralls YP gave me. My red beanie calls to me from the floor, but no municipal worker would ever wear one. I opt for one of Ma's baseball caps. We have a full-length mirror by the front door. Ma insisted on it: she likes to do a last look before heading out. My last look is solid. I really do look the part. Except for the whole sixteen-year-old-girl thing. And the striped socks thing.

Everything's ready. I go to put on my boots and—my boots. My breath catches in my throat, and I'm hit with this feeling. Not anger or disgust. Not fear, not nerves. *Doom*.

The doom hangs heavy in the front hall and keeps my eyes fixed on my boots, sitting on the bottom stair. The boots Mee gave me. Even after the expulsion, after all her disappointment, she never quit. She gave me a wall. *Who does that?* And what do I do to thank her? Lie. Over and over. The doom is suffocating me. The doom helps me decide. I can't do it. Not tonight. Not to Mee.

I leave my boots, bag, all my supplies, and head out to meet YP.

park near Dairy Barn and start walking toward the water tower. She'll understand, right? She's the only person who does. YP has to understand. I can't do it. We can do something else. We don't have to respond.

I keep chanting it over and over in my head. *She'll understand, right? She's the only person who does.* I pass the whale. *She'll understand, right? She's the only person who does.* I pass the school. *She'll understand, right? She's the only person who does.* Walk through the overpass. *She'll understand, right? She's the only person—*

Her arms wrap around me and squeeze so tightly I might pass out from air loss. She pulls back, hands on my shoulders, and smiles. I don't want to break her heart. But I'm sure she will understand. *She's the only person who does.*

YP takes my hand and leads me under the tower. I look up and imagine it buckling, crashing down on top of us both. Doom. We make it to the ladder and she offers her hands for a boost. This is the only time I've seen her look like a cheerleader since that day she decided to talk to me for the first time.

"Come on! We can't waste any time!" She bounces her hands, fingers interlocked forming a step up to the ladder overhead, demanding I place my foot there.

"Wait a minute. Please."

"Hey, you OKOK?"

"No, I'm not." I slink down to the ground and she kneels beside me.

"Hey," she waves. "It's scary-looking, but I know you can do it."

"How?" I twist my fists together.

"Are you kidding? You shouldn't————a pep talk! Look————-—————-you've done so far. This is your life, your art! Remember?" She brings her thumbs together.

"But this?!" I point up above us. "It's too much." She should recognize that. I didn't come here to argue with her. I didn't think I would have to.

"Not for you."

"Yes, for me! I'll do something else. Somewhere else. Another time. I just can't." My skin feels tight and itchy, it's not just the cold. I need her to be okay with leaving. What happened to Little Miss Rule Follower?

"Take a deep breath, okay? You can't quit."

"Why not? You quit Cheer."

"I never gave a shit about Cheer. This isn't about me." Her forehead crinkles as she curses. She looks furious. She shouldn't be mad at me; she should be mad at my rival writer. She's supposed to be on my side.

"I know! It's about *me*. How am I supposed to do this? What's next? The Empire State Building?" Her anger is contagious. I wrinkle my forehead to match hers.

"You're signing too fast!" she says as I steamroll ahead.

"Try to understand, it's only going to escalate until someone gets caught. I can't have it be me! Please—"

"Stop saying *can't*. You can!" she signs.

"How? How can I get up there, do this? All the pressure is on me! Not you! Back off, okay?"

"Back off?"

"I mean—"

"Me help you! I know how to get it done!"

"How? How can you possibly know that?"

"Because I did it."

"You?!" I yell, stabbing my finger at her. "The whole time?" YP stands still and exhales. She nods.

"Of all the idiot people in the whole fucking world, *you* did this to me?" It doesn't matter if she can't understand what I'm saying. My fear and anxiety twist into a deep dark rage. I can't believe it's happening again. Another knife lodged into my back, right next to the one Jordyn left.

"I didn't know it was you." YP arches her eyebrows, pleading for me to believe her.

"Bullshit. Maybe that first time, yeah. Sure. But you can't say that for the others. I told you! I told you it was me!"

"Too fast!" she signs again, tearing up.

"How could you do this to me?" I ask again.

"I didn't want a war. I thought the art looked great together. They fit together." She twists the knife.

"You think I'm talking about the stupid graffiti? Are you seriously as dumb as you look? You lied to me. Over and over. To my face."

"What sign this?" YP asks and repeats the sign for *liar*.

"L I A R. Liar, liar, liar. Every day since I met you has been one big L I E."

"Not true!"

"Oh, really? How many times did we talk about who the other tagger was? How many times could you have just come out with it?"

"I not want you to hate me!" she signs through pitiful tears. I don't feel one speck of guilt over them.

"How can I hate you when I don't even know you? Who the fuck *are* you?"

"You do know me! You know me better better better," she signs. "Don't be like this."

"Don't act like you care all of a sudden," I tell her. YP stiffens, her expression shifts from grief to bitterness.

"I care! I dropped out of art class last quarter so you could have my spot." She stands there, arms crossed, proud of herself. I'm disgusted. It takes me a second to respond to this newest low. I had her so wrong. Not only does she disrespect my art, my friendship, she pities me. I won't have it.

"How. *Dare*. You."

"What?!"

"Poor deaf girl can't get into art class! I know, I'll be the better person and help her out and take a knee so she can go use her magical deaf art powers." I use my voice, make her listen to how stupid she must sound when she talks. "Like . . . um . . . like blind people and music."

"I did it 'cause you're my *friend*." Of course YP starts sobbing. For once I don't feel bad for her. She brought this on herself.

"You're not my friend. Never were."

She knows better than to follow me right now. At least I hope she does. She was right about one thing. I do hate her. Hate, hate, hate her. I flick my middle fingers out from my thumbs again and again. *Hate hate hate hate.*

This whole time, patronizing me with her fake ignorance. *Oh, wow, graffiti, street art, so cool.* Signing that stupid-ass oath. Of course she knew who Banksy was, of course she suggested wheatpaste. She told me about the underpass tag— what, *moments* after *she* tagged it? She wasn't afraid of my reaction—she was playing me. *Hate hate hate hate hate.* I break into a run past Finley.

It wasn't Mr. Katz. He just really likes my art, that's all. Maybe he didn't even know it was me. I never gave him that sketchbook, I got so wrapped up in all this. Maybe I should give it to him after all. *UGH. None of this matters right now, Julia.* I head toward Lee, fists balled up, knuckles white.

This. Is. What. You. Get! I slam my fists onto the steering wheel over and over. What you get when you give a fuck about anything. I'm sobbing so hard I expect puddles of tears to rise up to my ankles. I should have known better, especially after Jordyn. How long has it been since she fucked me over, a semester? I should have learned my lesson, not gone confiding in some lame, cheery-cheeked cheerleader. Snot starts dripping from my nose, and I do my best to sniff it back up. Crying's disgusting. I'm a mess. Who cries over graffiti, anyway? My neck is cold and wet; I wipe away what I can with my sleeves. I want to drive home but I'm too upset. If I get pulled over and have to open the car door, a wall of tears will flood out like in those drunk-driving ads. And on New Year's Eve I doubt the cops will believe it's tears.

Fuck it. Fuck them all. I get out of the car. A boiling, snotting, dripping mess, I head to the Little League field.

There it is, the big whale and bones. The sight of it makes me want to scream again. This never would have happened if Casey didn't try to force me into friendships. I don't *do* friends, I don't do *friendly*. I don't play nice, because I get played. *That bitch.*

The whale glares at me, taunting me. Showing off. I trudge through the snow on the field, my feet freezing in my old, worn-out sneakers. Fuck footprints. I don't give a shit anymore. Come and find me. I'm responsible. With each step, my nostrils burn from anger mixed with the icy air.

The whole time. She knew the whole time, every conversation laced with lies. What did she think was going to happen?

High fives? Hugs? Was she *ever* going to tell me? Oh, my God, what if she never said anything?

The paint pen is in my hand before my brain realizes it's there. My arm starts writing before I even know what I want to write. You can write a lot faster when you don't care how it turns out—I'm back on the road in under thirty seconds, paint dripping and drying in the darkness.

Lee obediently waits for me, alone in the parking lot. Good. I'm finally ready to get as far away from here as I can. A car drives past, headlights sweeping across the pedestrian-crossing sign. Something in my memory sparks. The scoreboard *wasn't* the first time! That day, when we walked past drinking iced tea. The skeleton on my tag, the X-ray of the crossing man. I knew *then* that war was brewing. She pulled me away without saying a word.

(▲＿◢)

Donovan tastes like Mountain Dew and sweat. It's gross, but good: I don't want to enjoy it. Not too much, anyway. He moves his hands up my shirt, and I hit my head on the roof of his car.

"Your hands are *freezing*," I mime, and slide his hands under my ass for warmth. I can feel him laugh through the kisses. I knock off his visor and toss it into the backseat before I run my fingers through his blue-black hair. He tilts his head back and I kiss his neck. He's moaning; I feel his throat buzzing.

His car is a dump. I can count at least six soft-drink cups from where I'm sitting. Not to mention all the grease-stained bags, some clearly containing half-eaten no. 3s. It's more than a turn-off. I grind into his lap; he holds on to my hips and slips his salty-sweet tongue back into my mouth.

I close my eyes and try to imagine that it's months ago. That Jordyn never went out with him. That she let me have him after she got me expelled. That he approached me first. Back when I was crushing hard, when Donovan could do no wrong. Why couldn't he have given me the magnets then? Why did he only start liking me when he was already attached? I thought I could have been the exception. What a fool I was. What a fool he is.

I lift up my shirt and let my hair fall down over my

shoulders. His eyes light up and he greedily reaches for my breasts, arm hairs all smooth and perfect. I kiss him again and he closes his eyes. *Good*. I keep one hand on his chest while I use the other to wiggle my phone out of my back pocket. While he's busy kissing my neck, I hold the phone out behind him just high enough to fit us both in the frame.

"Thanks," I sign to him before reaching for my shirt.

"Wait, don't go. Not yet." He hangs on to my hips, his eyes search my face and my body. He's hoping for more.

"Sorry," I sign, getting out of the car. "Got what I needed."

"What?" He looks so stupid sitting there in the passenger seat. All worked up, no idea what's about to happen. I'd pity him if it weren't his own damn fault.

"I might be a liar," I sign with one hand, drafting a text with the other. "But at least I'm not a cheater."

Message sent.

(≧ 🏛 ≦)

The snow is melting; traffic lights reflect in the road on the way back to Finley, Red Bull nestled between my thighs. It's like my first day all over again. I won't fuck it up this time, though, that's for sure. Late last night I considered getting myself expelled again, but where would I go? Getting expelled again would destroy Mee. So, fresh start at Finley it is.

Bundled up, hands tucked under her armpits, Casey waits for me at the entrance to the school. *Crap*. I forgot to ask for a new terp. Maybe I can talk her into quitting. And by "talk her into" I mean "torture her into," obviously.

"Julia!" she signs, and waves. I keep walking. "How was your break? Did you do—" I stop her hands.

"Are you interpreting for anyone right now?" I ask.

"Um . . . no."

"Then you don't need to be talking to me." I blow past her toward my locker. Why do the slow fade when you can do the torch-and-burn? My locker springs open and I hang my coat up. My breath catches. I only notice it when I go to shut the door. She was here.

I want to laugh, not because YP's cheered me up or brought me around, but because she doesn't know how pitiful the gesture is. *Give it up.* The pink letters catch the light as I start to swing the door closed. I can't believe she thinks this is the way to handle the situation: breaking into my locker and tagging over my work yet again. Showing me up.

My new schedule commands me to head over to the math hall for intermediate algebra. Math's not too bad; numbers I can handle. The rules are the same no matter what language you speak. And bonus, Casey hates math. Lots of fingerspelling, lots of numbers. Not a lot of fun for someone who became an interpreter because *sign language is so beautiful*. Few people could make solving for x beautiful in any language. Definitely not Casey.

"You didn't see it yet, did you?" Casey asks, taking her spot next to the chalkboard.

"See what?" I reply with the stink-eye instead of words.

"Your English class," she signs without making eye contact. The schedule peeks out from the pages of my textbook. I slip it out, and lo and behold, I've been moved to ESL. *Shit.* I would say I tried, but I didn't, really. Here's the part where I would normally fly off the handle, rage against the English machine and all that. But after everything that's happened, *who cares*?

The first half of the day I spend zoning, fuming, working, and figuring out what the hell I'm going to do next. I point to a soft pretzel in the lunch line and fill a little paper cup with mustard. It's still bitter and cold outside, but I haven't run into *her* yet, and I don't plan on it. The concrete table in the courtyard is my new lunch hangout. I sit with my back to the windows. They can see me, but as far as I'm concerned, I'm eating my snack in Siberia. Alone.

I want to go out, I want to bomb every wall, every sign, every lamppost. I don't care if she was here first. She doesn't get to win this war. She won't be able to walk a single block

without a reminder of her betrayal, her crimes against whatever friendship I thought we had. Friendship. Friend*shit*.

I know it's Casey tapping my shoulder; I don't have to
turn around to know it's her, but I oblige. Her nose is already
running from the cold. *Toughen up.*

"Come inside." She motions to the door.

"Are you interpreting for someone right—"

"Stop it with that; look, I know ESL sounds bad, but—"
We take turns cutting each other off.

"I don't care about ESL."

"Oh, then why . . ." Casey looks me over, searching for the
right words.

"Unless you're out here, interpreting for a teacher or something, I don't see how it matters to you."

"Of course it matters—"

"Let me put it this way: it's none of your business. I'll
see you in class." I turn back to my pretzel and she takes
the more-than-obvious hint to leave. I wish I was a smoker. I
feel stupid sitting outside with nothing to do but look at my
busted-ass phone. Jordyn has texted, but I haven't replied
yet. Not much to say to her anymore. Soon she'll wise up and
leave me alone and I'll finally be invisible at work, too. No
way Donovan's ever looking at me again. They deserve each
other.

My butt starts feeling numb from the cold concrete bench.
I look over my shoulder and notice the cafeteria has emp-
tied. *Damn it!* Now would have been more helpful to butt
in, Casey. I have Mr. Katz next, and I'm sure she wants to be
there even more than I do.

.   .   .

The halls are clear as I rush to the art wing. This is bad—how late am I? It's the first day of the new quarter, so hopefully I'm not the only one. I pick up the pace. The door to Room 105 is closed. *Weird.* He never closes the door during class. I turn the knob and the whole class stares as I creep through the doorway.

"Sorrysorrysorry," I sign. Mr. Katz looks less than pleased at my late arrival. He points to an empty chair. Casey leans against the display wall and glares at me. It's okay. I made it. Everyone gets to be late on the first day of new schedules, right?

"I think it sucks," good ole Black Shirt says. He's back for more art this quarter. I survey the room. Black Shirt, Freckles, Pigtails, and YP. Wait. *What?* Our eyes meet and I immediately look away.

"What sucks about it?" Mr. Katz asks him.

"Why ruin a good thing? It was cool before, now it's all messed up," Casey interprets for Black Shirt.

"Is it any different than what the first artist did?" Katz continues his line of questioning.

"Duh." Are they talking about what I think they're talking about? Black Shirt continues. "It's like what she said." He points at me and I don't appreciate the second round of stares from the whole room. "What they did didn't add anything to the art. They had crappy intentions."

Ugh, using my own words against me like that. Gross.

"How do you know?" I sign at him. He looks at me when he answers this time.

"C'mon, did you see it? It's totally ruined." He actually looks at me when he speaks.

"Who says it's ruined? Who are you to judge?"

"You're joking, right? I can't tell with your, like, lady over there. You can't say it's better now than it was before."

"I think it was better when it was just a whale. Everything after that ruined it." I can feel YP staring at me from the other side of the room. My eyes want to look, too, but my willpower holds out. Casey starts interpreting again.

"You're wrong." I can guess who said that. I keep my eyes fixed on Casey.

"What makes you say that?" Katz asks.

"It was good," Casey continues interpreting. "The whale. And the skeleton? That was good, too. But together? They're awesome. Brought up to another level."

"Who are you to say?!" I turn and sign to YP. "Why are we talking about this at all? It's art class!"

"It's street *art,*" Pants emphasizes.

"It's not meant for some stupid roundtable discussion about what counts as art, or what's good and what's bad. Let it be what it is!"

"And what's that, Julia?" Mr. Katz tries to call me back down to earth with his question, but I'm too far gone.

"It's over. I'm done with this class." I grab my bag and slam the door behind me on my way out.

(ง่͏͏ᴖ̀͏͏ψ)ง

I don't care about still lifes and draperies, so what do I need advanced art class for? Nothing. I have everything I need right here. The basement is covered in papers and pencil shavings, left over from what was once the Big Plan. I sit cross-legged in my armchair and look over the sketch wasteland. When I snap to, Ma is staring at the floor alongside me. I don't shove the papers away. It's too late, she's already seen it all. At this point, I hardly care. This piece is never going up anywhere. It'll only ever live on paper. Nothing to see here.

"You're home?!"

"Obviously," she says, eyes fixed on the floor.

"What's wrong?"

"I should be asking you that." She sits on the arm of the chair next to me.

"Why?"

"I heard you quit art class."

"Casey needs to stop calling you, it's not fair—"

"Why would you quit art class?" She stares off into the room, not waiting for my answer. "I kept asking myself that. You really wanted to be there. You *needed* it after—after everything." I know better than to interrupt her. "So, why would you quit? Either something happened, or . . ." She sighs and motions to the floor. "You're back at it again."

"This? No, this isn't that." It was, but it's destined for the trash now.

"Don't lie to me, Julia." Ma picks up one of the loose pages. "If you quit class, what's all this for?"

"I'm allowed to draw on paper, aren't I?"

"Don't get defensive. Can't you tell me why you dropped out?" She releases the paper and it floats back to the ground. I want to tell her it's none of her business, that once again she's overreacting to information fed to her by an overreaching terp. I can't tell her about YP and me; she'll tell me to deal with it, stay in class, keep my commitment, don't let teenage drama keep me from my education, blah blah blah.

"Julia, I know these aren't for Mee's store wall." She indicates the piles of papers and pens. I've never wanted to be alone so badly in my life. I change tactics.

"Didn't Casey tell you? I got moved to ESL. No time for art if I want to pass."

"Really?" Ma digs her fists into her hips. This is her thinking-with-purpose stance. She stares off at some distant spot on the wall. "It's not something else?" She looks at the papers again, and the corners of her mouth turn down. I can tell she doesn't know if she should believe me, but I don't feel panicked. I feel empty. It's not like I'll ever use the plans, nothing here is worth the interrogation.

"I honestly thought that you—"

"Really. I'll take art next year or something. Whatever."

"Are you sure? Because I'm not so sure you need ESL. I could call the school and—"

"Ma! I'm fine, everything is fine, okay?" I flick the *K* hand shape at her. I thought I was done getting the third degree.

"Okay, Miss Attitude. Dinner soon."

Once I'm sure she isn't coming back, I pull out the very last of what was once my stash. After I got caught at Kingston, I got rid of nearly everything I had at home and opted for the new routine, the shell game with my black bag in different lockers. There's only one small box left. You wouldn't know it's contraband by the looks of it, which is why I kept it around.

I'm sure if Mee or Ma ever found the box, they'd assume it's just a bunch of empty glue pens. They don't scream *graffiti material,* not when they're empty. I can feel Ma walking around above me in the kitchen. I didn't tag the water tower, but I didn't exactly stop. I haven't stopped lying, I've stopped caring. Am I any better than YP? Maybe everyone on earth is a liar.

I'm not the cops, I'm not her dad. I'm her friend. I *was* her friend. That is what makes it unforgivable. She had no reason at all to lie to me, and I have every reason in the world to lie to my moms. I dump the contents of the box into my backpack and gather the papers off the floor.

Screw planning, screw big thoughtful pieces. I don't need planning. I don't need respect. I need revenge.

(ᵕ_ᵕ)

The bass blasts so loud in my car, the seats vibrate with every beat. I haven't turned on the radio in a year, maybe more. Tonight I need the distraction. *THM THM THM,* the steering wheel hums under my fingers. I don't want to think my way out of this one. I turn the knob up a little more.

Plans are for pussies. For toys who are afraid of getting caught. I don't need a disguise or an alibi. All I need is some paint and a wall. Everything else is a distraction from the real deal.

I roll through Dairy Barn. The cashier, frowning at the music, hands me a huge Styrofoam cup of iced tea.

"It's late!————down!" he yells, turning an imaginary knob. I wave and pull away into the parking lot across the street. I don't want that guy to think I'm lowering the volume for him, but I have markers to fill, so I shut off my car and the bass thumping ceases. The best thing about mops is you can fill them with craft-store acrylics. The watery stuff that grammies use for stenciling birdies onto flowerpots and bathroom walls works best.

No one gives you a second look when you buy the paint for this stuff. Even so, I gave up on mops a while back; they drip more and don't mix well. Generally, they're harder to control and don't make anything nearly as beautiful or perfect as spray. But I'm not looking for perfection anymore. Perfect is the enemy of getting it done. Right now.

First, I unscrew the caps and squeeze the paint from their tubes into the pens. A little bit of the Martha Stewart's Pursed Red Lips color dribbles onto the passenger seat. I try to rub it off with my sleeve but that only scrubs it deeper into the fibers. And now it's on my shirt. *Whatever*. I put the mops in my coat pockets and lock up Lee.

I bet I could walk from Dairy Barn to the underpass backward with my eyes closed at this point. How many times have I made this trip? I have to start switching it up, I can't keep tagging in the same places. Gotta expand, move on.

How did she do it? How did YP have me fooled for so long? Not just her innocent act—the logistics of the whole situation baffle me. She knew where I bombed, when I bombed. She retaliated so swiftly, but her art looked like it took weeks to plan. It doesn't seem possible that she could live all those lives at once.

I'm supposed to be the one you'd never suspect. I should be able to write at lightning speed, with no pauses for planning. No time for second guesses. How did a bouncy blond babe beat me at my own game? My fingers wrap around one of the mops as I walk under the overpass, each one filled with a different shade of gory red.

YP can suck it. Jordyn can suck it. Donovan, Casey, they can suck it. The red paint drips down the wall as I work over the mural. *Huh*. Two hearts, she put two hearts in the skeleton. She wasn't toying with me enough. Had to leave a little hint in there. I mop on a deep-burnt-red broken heart over one of the originals. I leave the other one untouched.

I use the brightest red for crossing over the eyes and let every drip run its course to the ground. Does she really expect me to forgive her? I scrawl the last few letters up and run the mop across the length of the wall as I leave.

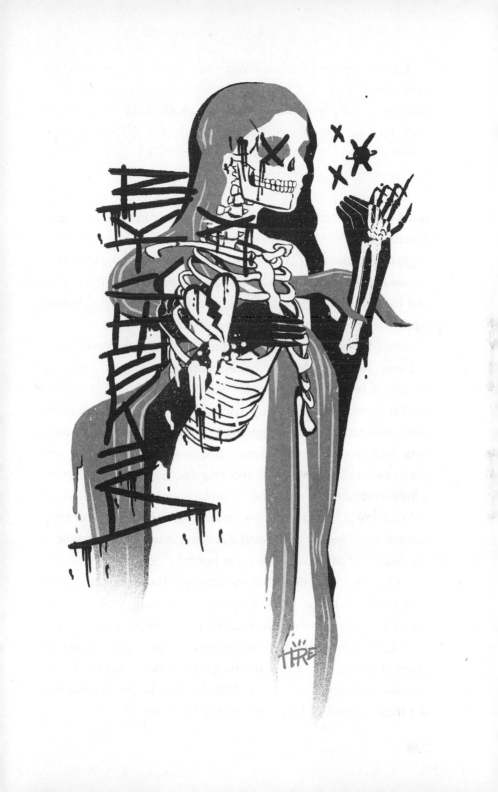

/(.□)\⌒Y°益°Y⌒/(□.\)

"I don't understand why, though!" Jordyn signs, during our break.

"Does it matter?" I need to quit this job. I'm exhausted by all the drama. I thought what I did would finally put an end to it. That they would both hate me so much, they would finally, finally leave me alone.

"Yes! It does!" She blocks me from leaving the room.

"You were worried he would mess around, so . . ."

"No, I wasn't!"

"Why did you ask me to stay away from him?" That shuts her up for a second. "What did you see in Donovan, anyway?" I don't know what I saw in him, either. The only thing I see now is that they are perfect for each other. Users. People who love you when you're new and shiny or when they need you for help, but the minute you need them—they vanish. They should get married, and divorced, and married again.

"I liked him!"

"You like everyone! *I* liked him, and you got bored and decided to swoop in."

"That's not—" Jordyn stops herself, she looks up to the ceiling and exhales. I can't tell if she finally understands me, or if she's plotting some new way to get my sympathy.

"Look, you wanted to know if he was a cheater, and now you know. I did you a favor."

"Jesus, Julia. You're so fucked up. I'm tired of pretending to be friends with you." She blows past me to the kitchen.

"So don't," I sign to the closed door.

I'm fucked up *because* people like her stab me in the back all the time. If everyone left me alone, I'd have nothing to be fucked up over. I straighten my black polyester collar and catch my reflection in the mirror on the wall.

I look *wrecked*. Like I need five hundred hours of sleep to make up for the past two weeks. My eyes are sunken in and darker than usual. I'd feel crappy about it except they remind me of someone's. They have that same tired look as *his*. That day when I pulled him off the fence, he looked ragged, but like a pro. I stand a little taller, thinking he and I might have more in common than I thought.

I flip off Donovan every chance I get. Granted, it's only in my head so I don't get canned, but I like to think he can feel it in the air. I'm sure I'm getting the same treatment from him, what with the death stares and clenched fists. Without Jordyn or Donovan to worry about, I'm on top of my game tonight. I got fries lined up for days. Evening rush? Bring it on.

"Your shift's over." The manager taps me on the shoulder and motions for me to leave. "Nice work tonight."

Wasn't expecting that. I raise my head high and smile on my way into the locker room. I don't need anyone to tell me I've done a good job, but I can't say I mind.

I'm all changed out of my grease-coated uniform when Donovan bursts into the room.

"You think you're funny?"

"No." I duck my head and click my lock shut.

"You realize——-——fucked over the only two————-liked you————place."

"You fucked yourself over," I sign.

"I can't understand you,——talk, damn it!"

"Ha!" I cough out for him to hear. I grab one of the mops still in my coat pocket and go up to his locker.

$$(\circ \wedge °)$$

"**Y**ou done being pissed yet?" YP signs to me, this time in the locker room. She's in three of my classes *and* has the same lunch period. I swear, it would be so hard to avoid her if I was a hearie. Thankfully . . . I turn my back and it's like she's not even there.

"——on, give it up————-." She moves in front of me. I close my eyes as I pass her on my way out. No, I'm not giving up that easily. The fact that what she did to me still doesn't strike her as a big deal only strengthens my resolve. I'm not the kind to kiss and make up; she should know at least *that* about me.

The gym is set up for indoor volleyball. I'm relieved to find that I'm not placed on a team with YP. Forty minutes of hitting a ball back and forth over a net and I'm out of here. I get to zone out in ESL, then eat lunch in my igloo. The feeling of relief doesn't last long. I feel it slip away as the ball rushes toward my face.

Stars flash and everything goes black. I feel a pop in the bridge of my nose that sends pins and needles shooting across my cheeks, as if the ball was slammed into the funny bone of my face. It's a shooting pain followed by numbness.

Am I bleeding? My hand rushes up to my nose and comes back dry. I'm fine, but damn, it hurt enough to be bleeding. I look up and Kyle Fucking Stokers glares at me. A chill runs over my arms. I signal that I'm okay to Ms. Ricker and the game continues. I'd expect KFS to high-five a bro, giggle over hitting the retarded girl in the face again. This was different. He wasn't joking, he wanted to hurt me.

I spend the rest of class avoiding the spike zone and generally trying to be out of the way. My nose is still throbbing— one more hit like that and I'm sure it'll break. *What's his problem?* Up until now, KFS has escaped my wrath entirely. I kind of forgot he existed, to be honest. I suppose it's possible he's truly a psycho and wants to screw with me because he can. I wouldn't put it past him.

YP must have gotten dressed fast, because there's no sign of her when the bell rings. *Good*. I get changed in peace, take my time, and drag my yellow boots to ESL. I assume Casey is already there and waiting, no more hallway walk-and-talks. Nice to know at least she's catching on. I pass the art room and Katz's red flannel catches my eye through the window. He looks so serious, talking to YP, who stares at the floor and picks at her nails. I try to read her lips but they're in profile and obscured by her hair. Mr. Katz must have felt me watching, because he looks up and frowns. I book it down the hall.

What a weird day. It'll be over soon. Everyone will stare and scowl and frown for now. But soon they'll stop caring, just like me, and I can go back to life under the radar. The ESL teacher gave me a sheet to evaluate where I'm at. Essay-type questions, so Casey is looking bored. The first question is about my influences. I know I can't write about Banksy or Swampy or Miss Van. Not with Katz talking about street art down the hall and my paint still drying on the underpass. What do they *want* to hear? I'll write about Mee and Ma. That should count for something.

Who are the most influential people in your life? How have they contributed to your life?
I think my moms are the most influential people in my life right now. They are good role model because even when they don't get along they still love together. They had to overcome a lot because one, they are Deaf, and two they are together.

While I'm writing, the teacher stands next to my desk and looks over my shoulder. Casey stands by, hands at the ready. The teacher addresses her.

"Can you tell her to stop? I'm going to help her."

Casey tells me to stop, then explains that Teach can talk directly to me. I'm not sure he gets it.

"So"—he takes out a red pen from his pocket and starts marking up my unfinished answer—"this isn't too bad. Here."

I think my ~~moms~~ Mom ~~are~~ is the most influential ~~people~~ person

"Hey!" I wave for him to stop. "I have two moms."

"Oh. Uh. Really?" He raises his bushy eyebrows at Casey.

"Really," we both sign/say at the same time. Casey smiles at me. I'm a stone wall. The bell rings and Mr. T practically shouts at me. There's no way I could understand his distorted mouth shapes without Casey interpreting.

"Sorry about that! Take the paper home with you, bring it back next class. O-kay?!"

Shout all you want, Mister. I ain't gonna hear you.

. . .

This has to stop.

The parking lot is full of kids getting in their cars, leaving. All the little fishies swimming home for the night. How in the ever-loving world did YP pull this off during school hours? I noticed it before I even stepped off the sidewalk. I'm stuck pacing back and forth from the curb to the flagpole, hoping each time the heart will be gone. It never is.

Of course. I pick at one of the edges of the heart: wheatpaste. I was so oblivious. She was dropping hints left and right. She should have told me. I can't relent now. I expected this from nearly everyone else in my life. But not her. She needs to understand that. I look down at the heart. Doesn't she get it? She broke mine.

Everything's playing out pretty well. Casey stopped bugging me; Jordyn and Donovan kissed and made up—both of them too bored or lazy to move on to someone new. I thought Jordyn would have stuck up for herself, but they deserve each other. At least they've stopped talking to me. I'm about 90 percent transparent, 5 percent visible to my parents, and for some reason, Katz is holding on to that last 5 percent.

I see him watching me watch everyone at lunch. I still sit outside every day, but now I face the windows, so I know when to head back to class. It's not that cold anymore. Either that or I'm growing thicker skin. I like watching everyone eat, mill around the cafeteria, through the glass. All the fish hanging out in the whale's guts. Throwing a party, oblivious that they were swallowed whole.

YP dumps her tray into the trash. I try not to notice it's full of food. I try to forget this is the fourth day in a row. Her tags have stopped. No more hearts, no more quotes. Nothing. *Weak*. If she really loved graff so much, she would be out there. She wouldn't let me stop her.

My tags are everywhere. Dripping red marks on the slide at the park, on the backs of stop signs. Some days it feels like I'm running out of places for it. It hasn't been easy. I avoid driving anywhere near my tags. I don't want people putting two and two together. I don't need to look at them anymore.

The fish stir in the whale's guts. Throwing away trash, hiking up their bags, and heading off to class. YP and Katz go to the art wing together. She's stopped checking over her shoulder for me when she leaves for class. She's stopped looking at me altogether.

Good.

$$(◎-◎;)$$

"**W**hy haven't you started yet? You told me you would start in February, and it's already March," Mee says. She takes her spot on the edge of my bed.

"I don't know what to paint," I tell her, and for once, it's the truth. I know the wall is there, free, legal, and all mine. But I can't bring myself to plan it out. It's too much work. Scrawling my new tag over every surface in sight is easier.

"No sketches? Nothing?" She looks around my room for any relevant scrap of art.

"Nope." I hang my head. I've disappointed her. Again.

"Ma said you had some out on the floor?"

"For something else."

"Something . . . illegal?"

"No! She already asked me that."

"I don't understand, Julia. Is it only fun if you're not allowed? Why shouldn't my wall count?" She swallows hard, and braces for my response. When Mee is worried, she takes deep breaths through her mouth. She's asked me to do the same thing when I'm upset. It tricks your brain into calming down. I've never gotten it to work for me.

"It's not like that."

"You aren't yourself lately."

"I'm always like this."

"Not true. Moody? Sure. Angry? Sometimes. But you don't smile anymore. You're a dark cloud."

"I'm fine." I'm so beaten down, telling her would just make it too real.

"Come and paint the wall, it will cheer you up."

"I told you. I'm fine." Mee wants to keep pushing the issue, but enough one-word answers force her to give in. I hate upsetting her, but I *am* always like this. I flop facedown on my bed. My nose collides with the mattress and I wince, the pain from the ball zings back into my sinuses. I let myself wallow for five more minutes. Life handed me a shitty year, and I want to roll over and sleep out the rest of it. But it won't help. Maybe I *should* paint Mee's wall; at the very least it would make her happy. And I can show YP just how fine I am without her.

I open my laptop. Maybe I'll find some inspiration online. My Hush*mail* has a bunch of junk I need to clear out. The forums spam my inbox a bunch, and I haven't been active on them in a long time. I log in and read. It's too risky to post on the thread I find.

SIBERxREBIS: wtf is up wit ths toy taggin evrywher? ne of u seen ths?

GNOMES: thaats fukked up. that first piece was tits. fuk toys earn ur stripes on stikies or somethin god.

T.HUB: ive seen that shit!

KORE: You've seen it? Who did it?

SIBERxREBIS: Kore gtfo we all kno ur a cop.

KORE: That is not true.

T.HUB: cop

GNOMES: cop

KEZTECK: cop

SOPROOAKS: cop

Fuck and double fuck. I've never been called out online before. Never posted pictures for this exact reason. Every now
and then some cop gets onto the forums and tries to squeeze
info out of toys. I am *not* a toy. These punks don't know who
I am. They look up to Neckface, but diss my new stuff? We're
not any different.

I read over the comments a few more times. They liked it.
Well, they liked it before my latest addition. It's better now.
They don't know what they're talking about. I don't regret it.
Not at all, so stop asking.

(ʋ _ belly)

Everything's been painted over. The scoreboard, the underpass. It's all gone. Most of the little tags I've thrown up
from Greenlawn to Queens have been covered or worn away.
Craft paint doesn't really hold up to the elements. My mops
are still there in my coat pocket, refilled and ready, but I
haven't found a decent spot since reading the forums.

"Hey! Pay attention!" Donovan shoves me and jabs a finger at my timer before pulling the fries out of the oil himself.
"Clock out before you burn the place down." His promotion
is going to his head. I don't stay to argue, though—I'd love to
get out of here early.

My phone buzzes after I get changed.

MEE: Will you be home for dinner?

Of course it's Mee, she's the only person who texts me
now. My phone has become this weird paperweight in my
pocket, my personal mom-communication device. I should
toss it. Be the only teen on earth without a phone. I let her
know I ate as I get into my car.

Lee's too obvious. She's probably attracting way too much
attention. The cops are stupid, but they aren't blind. I should
have painted her back to solid when I first saw them snooping

242

around the tunnel instead of tempting fate. *Let's go, Lee, time for a trip to the hardware store. You're getting a makeover.*

Buying spray paint might be off-limits, but I don't need it for what I'm doing. Lee is ancient. I love her, but her paint job doesn't need to be glamorous. I put some rollers—I'm saving the gifted ones from Mee for her wall—and a tray in my orange shopping basket and head for the paint aisle.

I'm trying to decide whether to paint Lee white or black when I see her. Quickly, I take two steps back and pretend to look at light-switch plates. I don't think she saw me. I peer around the corner, leaning far enough to see YP put a spray can in her own orange basket.

How does she plan on buying that? She's only two months older than me, and I know her birthday isn't until June. We had this whole birthday thing planned. *Whatever.* I watch her pick out two, three, four more cans before she's done. *What a haul.* I follow far behind her to the checkout counter.

Oh, look at these power-drill things, so reasonably priced. Just checking out tools over here, nothing to see. I'm certainly not stalking anyone. YP swoops her hair over one shoulder and saunters up to the cashier. He looks *really* happy to see her.

She puts her basket on the counter and leans over it, giggling, pushing her boobs together. The checkout guy checks out more than her paint. He turns red as she giggles again and bites her lower lip. I know this game. I used to play it with Mail Boy at Kingston. No, we aren't alike. We're nothing alike.

He doesn't ask to see her ID, doesn't even hesitate ringing her up. Puts the cans into a paper bag, and she's out of the sliding glass doors with a wave and a wink. A lady in an orange smock taps me on my shoulder.

"Can I help you——?" She gestures to the power tools.

"I'm good," I say out loud, and head back to the paints. I choose two big cans of dark gray enamel paint and use the self-checkout.

Everyone's asleep by the time I get home. The gate to our driveway is closed. I hop out of the car, leaving her running while I open the little chain-link fence.

We don't have any outdoor lights on the side of our house, but there's a street lamp that provides me with enough light to see what I'm doing. I'd rather paint her now, no one walking by, no one asking questions.

I pry open the first can with one of my keys. I forgot to buy paint stirrers, so I mix up the paint with a pencil before pouring some into a tray. The roller sops up some paint and I squeeze out the excess. Can't let it drip all over the driveway. Ma would kill me.

The paint rolls on in a thin coat; I'll probably have to go over her twice. I start with the trunk. I thought YP quit writing. I haven't seen anything around that looks like her work. There have been a few new tags popping up around school, but none of them are good enough to be hers. Where has she been painting?

I wrap around to the right side of the car, letting the roller do the work, rolling paint in W shapes so it doesn't streak too much. Maybe she's been planning this the whole time. I know what she's capable of, so I can't imagine what she'd pull off with months of downtime to plan. She did buy *a lot* of paint.

I roll back around over the trunk and to the left side of the car. She can do whatever she wants. She can go paint a huge piece and this time *I'll* tag over it. Then we'll be even. Except for all the lies. Can't forget that. I climb up on the hood to reach the roof. I keep climbing and take a break on the top of my car.

There aren't any stars here. When I go out writing in Greenlawn, they're always up. But not in Queens. The lights on Citi Tower and in Manhattan were my stars. Now, they aren't enough. The sky is a hazy, dark gray color; it'll be black soon. I dunk the roller into the paint well in the tray and finish up the roof. All that's left is the hood. I paint right over YP's heart in three big strokes.

Gray was a nice choice. Lee looks nearly invisible sitting in the driveway. Invisible car for an invisible girl. Perfect.

(◜ᴗ◝)

"We were going to pick up some pizza last night," Mee informs me as she fills a glass with grapefruit juice. "You must have gotten home late."

"Yeah, sorry. My phone's acting weird since I dropped it." It's sort of true.

"Where were you?" she asks as casually as she can.

"Hardware store. I gave Lee a makeover."

"You did?!" Mee rushes to the window and pulls open the little half-curtain. "Oh. It's . . ."

"Gray."

"So plain. I thought you might have done something more colorful, I guess."

"Nothing wrong with gray." I down my glass of grapefruit juice before grabbing my bag.

"I suppose not." She looks solemnly over the new paint job from the window. "Do you need some money for supplies? Is that why you haven't started on my wall? You know I'll get you whatever you need to start."

"I don't need money."

"What do you need?" she begs. There was a time when I might have taken advantage of this, but I can't take anything else from her.

"Nothing."

ᄆ(⊙＿⊙✕)

"**I**'m not sure I understand." Mr. T crosses his arms in front of his chest. "I don't think she needs to be in ESL . . . more like remedial English."

"Why not?" Casey asks him for me.

"She knows English! With her hands or something." He waves his arms around. I don't know who rolled their eyes first, me or Casey. She turns to me and signs, "Please."

"Fine." I give in. "Listen, English *is* my second language. I speak American Sign Language. It's not English. It's not charades, not miming. It's a language. How did you get to be a language teacher, anyway? I'm not so sure I can learn English from you." The smirk on Casey's face grows wider as she interprets.

"Excuse me?" Mr. T backs away.

"I don't think I need to be here either, honestly. But it's supposed to be your job to teach me, not to kick me out because you assume I already speak English. Would you throw out Philippe because he already knows English?" Philippe is the only other person in my ESL class. He's a tiny freshman with a bowl cut and a little shadow of a mustache on his upper lip. It's so ugly it's cute.

"Philippe doesn't know English!" Mr. T's face starts turning red. Philippe's eyes dart from my hands to Casey's to Mr. T's face. Clueless. "How am I supposed to know you're learning? You don't talk!" Mr. T argues.

"I don't need to—"

"Yes! In order to speak English, you have to SPEAK!" He must have really shouted. Casey looks stunned, and poor Phil looks scared out of his mind.

"I was saying—" I start in on a new rant, but Casey cuts me off. She stands in front of me; I can't see her face. Her gestures have nothing to do with sign language, that's for sure. Phil hooks his finger into his collar and pulls it away from his neck, as if to say, *Jeeeeez*. We both start cracking up. Both the adults turn back to us with furious faces. Casey tells me to get my belongings. We're leaving. I leave class first, with a little nod to Philippe. Casey ushers me in front of her before flipping off Mr. T through the window in his door. Her face is still curled into a snarl when she storms away. It's the most badass thing I've ever seen within the walls of a school.

"Where are we going?" I ask her as we hurry away.

"Don't know yet. Never done that before." She pulls on her scarf anxiously between sentences.

"Leave a class?"

"Curse someone out." She pivots back the way we came. "I should apologize."

"Are you kidding?" I keep pace with her so she can see what I'm saying.

"You're right." She swivels back. I think she's sweating. "He made me so mad! He's supposed to be a professional." She starts biting at the cuticle around her thumb.

"I get it."

"This was a mistake," she signs with her left hand, still gnawing at her right. "I wasn't ready for all of . . . this." She gestures at me.

"You're fine, Casey."

"Um . . . no, Julia, I'm not."

"He's an idiot! You were right!"

"Not right to say what I said. How I said it! Oh, God." She starts pacing again.

"Just relax!"

"Relax?! I'm going to get fired—for what? For you? You don't even like me!" We face each other in the hall. Casey stares me down, panic-stricken, waiting for me to say something. But I can't. I don't know what to say. She's right, isn't she?

She turns her back to me and changes directions twice more before deciding to go into the main office. She shuts the door before I can follow her inside.

Students flood the hall between periods. Casey still hasn't left the office. I wonder how long I should wait for her. I wish I knew what she said to Mr. T; it must have been pretty harsh. Damn, that would have been fun to know. I work my way to my locker, slowly, giving Casey more time. If she doesn't come back soon, I don't know how I'll make it through the rest of my classes. I'm not voluntarily going into that office, though. I'll wait.

I unlock my locker but the door jams and gets caught on something. I pull harder and it jerks open. A paper bag falls to the floor. The folded top must have been crammed between the hinges of the locker. "Hey, HERE" is written on the front.

How does YP keep getting into my locker? I don't want to open the bag in the hall in front of everyone, but I'm growing more invisible by the day. No one's going to notice anything.

The contents of the bag:

Three spray tops: one stencil cap (fine lines), one pink dot cap (super-fat spray), and one gold dot cap (a happy medium).

A disposable respirator.

Black vinyl gloves.

A note written on a "Hello, my name is" sticker:

I put everything back in the paper bag and push it down into my black bag, which I've just started using as my normal, boring backpack. My folks have given up on the at-home inspections.

Why do I even bother locking this thing anymore? I slam the door shut before I realize I'm in the hallway by myself. The door to the office opens and the vice principal, I think, steps out. He searches around, catches my eye, and waves for me to come over.

"Your——is——-—so—say——to—tha—--ifthatsokaywithyou." He talks so fast and jittery I'm surprised I caught even that last bit. I take my phone out of my coat pocket. The screen has a big red splotch of paint on it. I try scratching it away with my nail. Seeing it sets something off in him. He pinches the bridge of his nose and points to the phone, annoyed.

"No phones—-a the——s—." He points to my cell one more time to drive his point home. I leave the paint alone for now and type into the notes app.

I do not understand you. i am sorry.

He takes the phone from me and his eyebrows arch up, his mouth makes an O shape, and he starts feverishly typing.

Your translator has quit. I asked her to finish out the day, but she refusd.

What i do now

Go to your classes.

How will I understand?

try fora bit someone else is on th way.

He hands the phone back to me and shoos me off to class in the wrong direction.

. . .

Going to class without a terp would be the biggest waste of everyone's time. I can't believe she actually left. That was the plan, get her to quit, but I didn't think she would really give in. She seemed tougher than that. I don't think I can even take the credit for what set her off anyway.

With her gone, nearly everything is going how I pictured it, with the exception of YP breaking into my locker. I wonder who can see me now. Anyone?

I stand as still as I can in the entrance of the school. Main doors in front of me, gym directly behind. Cafeteria to my left, office to my right. How long will it take for someone to notice me standing here, doing nothing?

I start pacing along the front doors, all the way around and back. I switch and go in the opposite direction. Still nothing. Everybody's in class. Pacing gets boring. I sit under the pay-phone bank. I wonder why we still have them. I've never seen a kid pick one up and use it.

I take out the paper bag again. There's no way I'm going. She can paint all on her own. I might go after, to see what she does, but I don't have to be there for it, or participate. Plus, I can't exactly copy her tactic for buying paint. Not so easy to flirt it up when you don't speak the same language.

Which doesn't matter, because I'm not going. When class lets out, I pace around and around again. Waiting for someone to bump into me or call me out for cutting. To yell at me to get back to class, to throw something at my head. Anything.

Nothing.

. . .

I did it. I'm actually invisible.

No one cares.

Perfect.

I take out one of my mops and tag both of the pay-phone receivers.

No one notices. I sit underneath them and sketch out more signs in the dictionary I'm sketching for Katz. I add the signs for *fire, liar,* and *hurt.* Being invisible is boring.

You know what, I'm not giving YP the chance. Or the satisfaction. I'm retaliating *right now.* Not waiting for the end of the week and the wee hours of the morning, to show up and be shown up. *This. Ends. Now.* I zip up my bag and stride toward the art room, invisible and unstoppable. I'm Julia. I'm on a mission. I'm HERE.

Unsure if there's a class in session, I approach Room 105 very slowly. The art gods, once again, shine down on me. The room is empty and dark. Most important, it's unlocked. This will only take a minute.

The door swings open and I beeline for the supply cabinets. I don't waste any of my attention on the latest art projects hanging on the walls. I'm here for only one thing. Paint.

Last time I took the first three cans I could reach. But this time, I'm putting an end to our war. It needs to be better than anything we've done together. I pull out a few more cans and inspect my color options.

I'm instantly drawn to a can of yellow. Old habits die hard. I shake it up. No good: I can feel it's almost empty. I'm going to need a lot. I'm not planning this one out. No more plans. I have to take the fluorescent orange, that's for sure. I shake it up and put it in my bag.

Shake-test a can of red, a can of teal. Take 'em. Shake up a can of white, take it. Shake up a—

The lights flick on and off, and the can of purple I was holding falls to the ground. Can I make it to the window? I don't want to turn around, can't bear to see the look on his face. The lights flash again. I'm frozen, breathing deeply, trying not to have a panic attack.

"Julia." Mr. Katz comes over to me and signs. His eyes, they stab me in the heart. I can't look at him.

"Julia, please . . ." He points to himself. I look up, my lip trembles. I'm mortified. I can see he is having a hard time figuring out how to talk to me. It's the longest minute of my life. Silence is the loudest sound.

"Where C A S E Y?" he finally asks.

"Q U I T," I tell him, head hanging down toward the floor. When I look up, he's no longer disappointed. He's pissed.

"Let's go." He takes my bag and gestures for me to follow him out of the classroom.

(↑_↑)

Mr. Katz didn't plead for leniency on my behalf, but he evidently didn't bring up the paint, and I'm sure as hell not about to. I could have sworn he told the principal that he would call my parents to address the situation, but that never happened. I would take a whole week of in-school suspension in exchange for sparing me from that phone call. I was only sentenced to a day. God bless you, Mr. Katz.

The only good thing about being stuck in ISS is that I don't feel the need to look for an interpreter until I'm released. I spent an hour here yesterday, sitting in utter silence with the temp terp they must have called in, phone obscuring his face all afternoon like Magritte's apple. Nobody's on my case to find a new terp until I wait out my sentence and I'm allowed to talk again.

I sit here in the tiny cell of a room, door open, across from the office. Alone. I was told to wait for a pile of work from my classes. So, I'm waiting. And waiting. They gave me a sheet with the rules so I don't get "confused."

IN-SCHOOL SUSPENSION RULES AND REGULATIONS
1. *No talking at any time.*
2. *You are permitted to do only the work provided for you by your teachers. If you do not complete the provided work, you will receive a zero grade for the day.*

3. *No reading.*
4. *No drawing.*
5. *No cell-phone use.*
6. *You will sit in your assigned seat with both feet in front of you, facing your desk.*
7. *You will keep your area neat and clean. Trash can be disposed of only on a break or at the end of the day.*
8. *You will be allowed to purchase a lunch. You must eat your lunch in the ISS room.*
9. *No other food, gum, candy, etc., will be permitted.*
10. *Bathroom and water breaks will be provided. If you must use the bathroom, speak to Mrs. Gomez. You are permitted to be in only the ISS room and the office.*
11. *Sleeping is not permitted.*

ISS is all about waiting and no gratification. I put my head down to wait for my assignments and Mrs. Gomez comes in and starts yelling at me, pointing at the intercom over and over. I take out a notebook and write out: "I AM DEAF. SORRY." She crosses her arms over her giant boobs and taps her foot.

"You——-—-can pretend——but I know——that never——ever—" I cut her off by waving the paper again. This time I speak, so she'll actually believe me.

"I'm really Deaf. I'm sorry." She turns three shades of red, and I sit a little taller having put my jailer in her place.

"Oh!" She raises her thick arms to make a desk and puts her head down on it. Then she wags her finger back and forth.

"No, no, no, okay?"

"Okay," I laugh as she bustles out the door.

Twenty minutes later, still no assignments. I count the

tiles on the floor. I count how many people pass by in green shirts. Blue shirts. Red flannel. Mr. Katz walks by ISS swiftly, glancing back over his shoulder as he disappears out of view. Making sure I'm there. I look up at the ceiling and count those tiles.

Mrs. Gomez is back, arms crossed, at the door. She looks down the hall and crooks her finger in the air as if to say, "Come here." She punctuates it by pointing at the floor, sharp and stern: "NOW." She holds out her hand, and Kyle Fucking Stokers reluctantly hooks his backpack over it. Mrs. Gomez tells him where to sit, shuffles in behind him, and hands him a copy of the same welcome-to-hell sheet. She opens his backpack and hands him one notebook and a pen from inside. The rest she zips back into the bag, which she brings into the office with her. I wonder what happened to my black bag.

KFS slams his notebook down on the desk and pushes the chair against the wall. He yells something at the door, spit flying from his mouth. A vein in his neck is raised and purple. It's intimidating. I try not to stare. Either Mrs. Gomez is using the intercom, or he's having a conversation with the ceiling, or God. Whoever it is, KFS is pissed.

"What're you looking at, retard?" I guess I am staring. I sign the word for *nothing* and look back down at my desk.

"Listen . . ." He gets in my face, pointing.

Before he can let it rip, Gomez is back in the room, scolding him. I can see why they put her in charge of the ISS kids. She doesn't stand for any shit. Except instead of yelling, she sort of scolds you, like a mom. A very strict, no-nonsense mom.

"You're————it worse, Kyle. I don' wanna————ackere———orrow, kay?" I bet she's got an accent.

257

"Whatever." KFS slumps in his chair.

"Good boy." Mrs. Gomez smiles and turns on her little kitten heel.

Eventually, someone drops off a pile of papers for me and another for him. I start on my math sheet. The rest of the papers look like busywork; they have nothing to do with what we've been working on in class. KFS sits staring at the door, not even looking at the stack of papers on his desk.

Isn't he bored out of his mind? Sure, I don't want to be sitting around filling out worksheets, but the alternative is staring into space for six hours. I wish I had that kind of resolve.

"You need the bathroom?" Mrs. Gomez asks from the doorway. Kyle practically bum-rushes her on his way out. I don't have to go, but a change of scenery would be nice, even if it's only toilets and sinks. Mrs. Gomez waits between the bathroom doors for us to finish before ushering us back to our cell.

My head hurts. I need caffeine. I slide my head down onto my history paper and close my eyes. This only lasts a moment before I'm jolted back into reality. KFS kicks my chair. "————head up, re-mem-ber?" I give him a thumbs-up.

"Shut up with that," he snarls.

"What?" I act out, raising my shoulders, arching an eyebrow.

"You know," he says.

"No, I don't." I shake my head.

He turns to face me and starts in on a rant, talking so fast I don't even try to lip-read. Instead I focus on his expressions, but he really exhibits only one. *Contempt*. I didn't get him sent here. I don't know why he's here with me. What's he so pissed at me for? I raise my shoulders again, trying to get him to stop. I hold up a finger and write out in my notebook:

I cant understand you

He rips the notebook from my hand and starts scrawling his response.

stop acting like your so fucking cool. your not. all you are is a bitch.

and youre a dick. what do you care anyway

i dont care about you at all. but if she gets sick again. thats on YOU.

Mrs. Gomez shuffles back into the room: it's time for lunch.

I thought having Casey sit with me at lunch was bad. This is so much worse. Everyone knows, and everyone gossips. We aren't allowed to go to the cafeteria and come back alone. Mrs. Gomez waits in the lunch line with us. Our ankles might as well be shackled together.

We both point to our selections. Even though KFS can speak, he doesn't. Mrs. Gomez chats happily with the lunch ladies and other kids in line. Everyone loves her. Everyone who's not in ISS, anyway. It feels like all eyes are on us when we leave the kitchen. I miss my little table outside, looking in.

I spot YP: floral-print yoga pants, white top, suit jacket. Her hoop earrings are so huge you could use them to hula. I hate that my first thought is: *Shit, she looks cool.* She doesn't have a lunch tray. She's texting or Tumblring, sucked into her phone. Frowning.

"What——-—-do, man?" a guy in a jersey asks KFS. He glares back, and the guy takes the hint. What *did* you do?

Mrs. Gomez chaperones us through lunch. Once we're back in our cell, I can see she's lecturing KFS, but not in a condescending way. She obviously cares: her gestures are gentle and expressions are soft. Every now and then I get a sympathetic glance, but nothing more.

Once she leaves, I flip open my notebook.

Shes not my responsibility

See you are a bitch. i knew you werent really friends with her

you dont know what you're saying. i was a really good friend for her.

then you ditched her or some stupid shit right?

how you know any of this

you got all friendly and fucking ditched her, and all im sayn is if she gets sick again its your fault.

MY FAULT? YOU DITCHED HER all because she got FAT. YOU BROKE HER HEART.

shut up

YOU broke up with her when she got FAT

fuck you

I throw the book at his chest. He stands up, his chair crashing into the desk behind him. He glares down at me. I'm not afraid, I stand straight up and meet him face to face. *Try me.*

"You," he spits, "you don't . . ." Kyle slumps back into his chair and looks up at me. "You don't————. It can't ---- me anymore." His eyes water, he turns away to hide them. Why wouldn't it be on him? He's the one who broke her.

I pick my notebook up off the floor and hand it to him.

She never had friends, she always hung out in the art wing doing her art thing whatever. No one gave a shit about her cause she was fat i guess? thats what she said to me. i took a class with her. i was like the only dude to ever talk to her. so she went and got herself all skinny and pretty and made cheer and friends. and she said she was happy, and i liked her and yeah we went out and shit. but i noticed that she never ate, and was always sick and she said she was happy but she wasnt.

He wipes his nose with his sleeve before going back to the note.

and one day she fainted at my house and it was just too much for me to handle. okay??? i have my OWN shit to worry about too you know? im not her dad im just a

261

guy. so i told her dad and he sent her to get help. but af-
ter that i was just done. she's a chill person or whatever
but i can't handle that. I didn't break up with her cause
shes fat. i dont give a shit if she weighs a fuckton. i got
her better and thats all i could do. and NOW you're
fucking it all up.

The rest of our ISS sentence flies by. It's 2:45 and we're reunited with our backpacks and cell phones.

"Be good——-," Mrs. Gomez urges as she locks the door behind us. Free to go. Thankfully, there aren't many students hanging around to stare, so we brave the halls on the way to the parking lot. I break away for my car, but Kyle stops me with a hand on my shoulder.

"What now?" I use my voice; I've had enough of him for a lifetime. Especially after today.

"Don't fuck it up." He thrusts his finger into my chest. I swat him away, ticked.

"Don't touch me, okay? Stop that. You understand me?" I'm talking to him out loud, my throat feels dry and scratchy.

"Yes." He backs off. "It's just—"

"I know."

"Do you?" He speaks slowly, wanting me to understand him. "Because I really did try to help her and—"

"I get it, but listen—" I start. "You listening?" Kyle nods but doesn't hesitate to roll his eyes. "I know you did what you had to do. I understand why. But that doesn't make you some kind of saint." I feel my voice catching in my throat on certain words, but he looks annoyed, which means he must understand what I'm saying. "You were horrible to me. All year. Awful. You don't get a free pass."

"Like you———a brat, too? Sulking———acting———
you're better——everyone else?"

"I didn't deserve—" I try to explain that he's partially to
blame for my attitude but he cuts me off with a wave. He lifts
his hand and slowly and awkwardly spells out:

T

R

U

C

E

He laughs, because my jaw must be scraping the pavement. Who in the whole damn universe taught Kyle Fucking
Stokers how to fingerspell?

"Doesn't———-kid learn———like, kindergarten?" he explains, reading my confused expression.

"Fine. Truce, for now."

I sit in my car, reading and rereading his note. Thinking
about YP, friendless in the art wing. What's so wrong with
that? Being alone isn't so bad. She's always been so sensitive.
I think about her being a cheerleader, surrounded by buzzing girls, boys crushing on her. Dating Kyle, of all people. Of
course she quit Cheer. She only wanted the friends, and those
friends sucked. I feel a small comfort in knowing I outranked
them in her mind.

It's not fair. Why should I be forced to give in because
she's delicate? She really did lie to me, I'm not making that
up. I didn't ditch her for no reason. I've been alone since then
and I've been—

No. I haven't been okay. *Shit*. We're both messed up.

After today, I think I've earned an iced tea. I pass three of my butcHEREd tags on the way to Dairy Barn. No wonder I've been avoiding these streets. They look like ass. What was I thinking? I have to go to 5 Pointz. Revenge or no revenge, I need to make up for all this garbage writing.

When I get my phone to type out my order, there's a text notification on the screen. The attendant is already waving impatiently at me. I flash my order on the screen, pay, and drive on through.

YP: this cant wait til friday, 5ptz NOW. something happened.

(*´ｏ̫ｏ̫) (´ｏ̫ｏ̫ `)

hit every red light on my way to the highway. I flip off each one until it turns green. She must be okay; she couldn't text if she was hurt. Or caught. Doesn't matter. I press down on the accelerator. I need to be there, *now*. I should be driving to work. I consider texting Donovan, telling him I'm sick, but I never want to text him again. Consider this my resignation. *Sayonara*, Mickey D's. Find someone else to deep-fry fat sticks. I'm out.

The drive is a blur: suburbs, highway, city. I park as soon as I see a spot. I won't find one anywhere close, so I lock Lee up, leave everything behind, and run.

There she is, flower print, suit jacket, and all. Blond hair draped over a silver backpack, a Nordstrom shopping bag at her feet. She's reading the "coming soon" condo announcement again. The building's been painted since we were here. No murals, nothing but white primer covering every surface, windows included. All the graffiti ghosted underneath the thin layer of white. *Fuckers.*

"Hey." She turns and waves sheepishly. She must've heard me coming.

"This sucks." I point up to the building.

"You didn't see it yet, did you?" she signs with complete confidence. She must have been practicing this whole time.

"No, I haven't been back. When did they paint it over?"

"Not this!" YP points over her shoulder. "This isn't why I texted you."

"What, then?"

She starts chewing at her nails. "I really am sorry, you *have* to know that," she explains.

"What you did, it broke my heart," I tell her.

"I know, mine was broken, too. I didn't mean—"

"I know." I cut her off. She looks so defeated. Tired. I really hope she ate lunch. Her shoulders droop forward, her jacket rumples, the sleeves dappled with pink paint. "Hey, is that . . . *his* jacket?" I tug at the sleeve.

"Oh, . . . uh . . ." She turns red. "Yeah."

"Ha! It looks good on you!"

"Listen, small or big, choose."

"What do you mean?" I ask.

"I have two things to show you. Small or big first?"

"Small, I guess. I'm not ready for anything too big."

YP swings her bag around front and unzips it. I catch a glimpse of school papers and books, but not much else. She pulls out a small flat package, rectangular and wrapped in pink wrapping paper, and hands it to me.

"It was in the coat," she says as I unwrap the paper. It's a Moleskine sketchbook—shiny, soft, and black. "I think you should have it." I flip through the pages. Oh, my God. It's *his*. It's his B-book.

"This is insane! You don't want it?"

"Well, I look so good in the jacket!" she signs, and twirls around. I can't help it. I swoop in and wrap my arms around her.

She gives me her death squeeze, but I don't care. It's not tight enough. I want us to get out of here. Hop in my car, head to her house, split ten pies and talk about nothing for a month straight. She pulls away too soon and sees that I'm crying.

"I'm sorry, too. Really," I tell her.

"You don't have to be."

"You know that's not true." I hug her again, and I can feel her laughing. I pull away and sign, "Thank you." We flip through the pages some more.

"This dude is magic," I tell her, and she hugs me again.

"I'm really glad you came. I didn't feel right stashing it in your locker. I wanted to give it to you."

"Oh! My locker! What did you want to paint? What happened?"

"That's the big thing. You ready yet?"

"Yeah, I'm ready."

This time, YP leads the way around the fence. I can just barely make out the old graffiti beneath the primer. Ghosts of writers past. It's depressing, and sort of spooky, thinking about how in a few years, no one will even know it was here. A whole gallery of graffiti, gone. When we reach the spot where we rescued the Suit, YP points up to the building, but I'm already looking. It's unmissable.

He came back.

"Did you . . . ?" I turn to YP, picking my jaw up from the concrete.

"You kidding? I can't do *that*!"

"How does he know we . . ." I spray invisible paint in the air.

"I have, like, literally no idea," she laughs. (She signs the word *like*. It's hysterical.) YP's hair glows orange in the setting sun. We both hang on the fence, saying nothing, smiling and carefully looking over every detail of his piece. He got us. I don't know how, but he did.

"Let's put him in his place." YP throws the jacket on top of the barbs and climbs up and over as if she's done it every day of her life. Piece of pie. "Hurry up!" She checks in both directions as I climb over the fence. She tosses me a can of Jet Black and vinyl gloves from her Nordstrom bag and we get to work.

YP is smart. No supplies in her backpack, everything in the shopping bag under a thick layer of tissue paper. She pushes a pink dot cap into place on a can of yellow and shakes it up.

"Hey!" I wave and get her attention. "You have M A G N E T S?" I point to the bottom of the can.

"What T O Y sold you on that trick?" she laughs.

"It doesn't work?"

"Most cans," she signs, "have G L A S S balls in them." Face, meet my palm.

Embarrassed, I uncap and walk to the wall. I reach my arm out, but YP stops me. She pulls a paper respirator over my nose and mouth.

"You need. Is important," she signs, before pulling hers down. Only YP would be worried about fumes when the clock is ticking. Never saw the point of a face mask, still don't. I hang back and watch her work first.

Her left hand clenches into a fist and relaxes a few times. She's deciding where to start. I can literally see her *Aha!*

moment in her body language. She rushes the wall and sprays two giant yellow circles over our likenesses' faces. *Oh, my God. I get it.*

I grab a stencil cap and hook it onto the collar of the black can. We can't have our faces up on a wall, a giant picture of us spraying. YP is smart. I add some smiles. We fall into a rhythm, each taking turns, watching the other, then adding our own touches. Once we've been at it for a while, we have to move faster. The politeness ceases and we go for it, moving quickly, trading places, swapping colors. We're a blur of color, painting until YP hears footsteps and we run like hell.

Everything gets put into the Nordstrom bag and tossed into the first Dumpster we pass. She doesn't save her paint. I want to keep running, but YP's practically window-shopping.

"You work so C L E A N!" I tell her.

"You work fast!" She snaps her fingers. I see her bike chained to a post near the 7 train entrance.

"You want a home?" I ask as she unlocks the bike. Her face goes white. She swallows hard. "What? What is it?"

"S T A Y C A L M," she spells quickly before turning around, face to face with two police officers. She smiles at them. I want to run. Everything in my body screams for me to get the fuck out of there. This time, my head knows better than my body. Running would only guarantee I'd get dragged in. I stand shoulder-to-shoulder with YP.

"What——-two girls——----- evening?" the bigger of the two cops asks. I can't make out what YP says. She's talking fast, grinning wide.

"Is——so?" the lady cop asks me. I slowly point to my ears and shake my head. YP steps in and tells them I'm deaf. The cops exchange a skeptical look.

"It's true," YP signs and speaks.

"We——-call————-girls————your description———————-vandalizing————-property."

"Sorry," YP signs/speaks. "We're coming from——"

"Hold——-————hands," Big Cop demands. YP starts to interpret but Big Cop cuts her off again. "I——, hold out——hands!" He mimes for me and I comply. Fem Cop flips our hands over, inspecting every crease and cuticle. Mine are sweating so much she has to wipe her own hands on her pants when she's finished. Our hands are clean, but she isn't satisfied.

"Open your bags," Fem Cop orders.

"I don't————-to——search," YP says, holding her bag.

"Good for you," Big Cop huffs, and snatches the bag from her. "So————you're here——-train station,——free—search you."

Oh, fuck. Is there paint in my bag? Mr. Katz *had to* have taken it back, right? I hand my bag over to Fem Cop. He wouldn't have left it in there. I feel a bead of sweat roll down my back. No, he *would* have. That's exactly the sort of thing Katz would do. He *likes* the art, but hated my behavior. Fem Cop unzips the front of my bag. I'm light-headed, I feel like I'm going to pass out. I take a breath, but it feels like I can't get any air in. Please, Katz, be a hard-ass. Just this once.

Fem Cop pulls out my notebook and busywork from earlier in the day and throws them on the ground. No paint. *Katz, I could kiss you.* I risk a glance at YP, who looks more annoyed than terrified. Her books and papers are also on the ground at her feet. I have no idea how she's staying so calm.

"Arms out." I do as Fem Cop says. YP does the same, but Big Cop takes a step back. Fem Cop runs her hands up my right sleeve and back down again. I'm going to throw up. I don't know how I'm still standing. I've dreamed of running from the cops, fooling them at every turn, with Pum Pum, with Creepy, with Wurstbande. In Buenos Aires, in Australia, in Berlin. But I can't handle it as she fem-handles my left arm. In this moment I don't pretend to be tough. I cry. The tears fall. They run and drip off my chin and onto my shirt. Fem Cop notices and takes a step back.

"What's——-got———-about?" she demands of YP. I've never been so scared and confused in my life.

"She doesn't know what's going on," YP signs, and explains, pointing to her ears. I sob. Big Cop laughs. His face is smug, punchable. He motions for Fem Cop to get on with it. She does. And I'm an idiot.

I'm an idiot for blowing up like I did, for tagging like a toy. For telling myself planning is for pussies. For lying to my moms over and over. I'm an idiot and I deserve everything that's about to happen when Fem Cop pulls out the blood-red mop from my coat pocket.

(͞π͞∩͞π)︿(͞π͞∩͞π)

"What's this?" Fem Cop holds the mop up in my face. All the color drains from YP's. She's so smart, she has all her bases covered. Here I am, the toy with paint in my pocket. I'm sinking us both. I start to explain, but Big Cop tells me to keep my arms at my side.

"Pen and paper," I say aloud. "I—I—I n-need a pen and paper."

"Finish first," Big Cop tells Fem Cop. She hands him the mop marker and pats down my legs before moving on to YP. YP is clean like Greenlawn snow. I'm as dirty as Queens sludge. She never has to apologize to me again. I'm the one who fucked us.

"So, what's this?" Fem Cop repeats herself.

"Pen and paper," I remind her. Instead of getting me a pad to write on, she turns to YP. So against the law, but the officer doesn't seem to care, or know. Fem Cop talks fast, her lips are thin and coated in gloppy gloss. I have no idea what she's saying. More tears cling to my chin, then drip to the ground. I don't dare lift my arm to wipe them away.

"You can't prove—-—that!" YP doesn't appear to be yelling, but she's nowhere near as calm as she was before. Big Cop doesn't care. He opens the back door of his cruiser, and ducks her head inside.

274

"Pen and paper! Pen and paper! Pen and paper!" I shout over and over. They have to give it to me. It's the law. I can't believe I thought cops who cut corners were only in movies and bad TV. Fem Cop ducks me into the seat next to YP. They take our school IDs and leave us in the backseat. We can see them through the windshield, talking into their radios.

"OKOK?" YP signs.

"No!" I shout. I put my face in my hands. So thankful they didn't bother cuffing us.

"Hey." She pulls my hands away. "It'll be okay. OKOK." She looks deep into my eyes with certainty.

"How can you say that? How can you be so calm?" I demand.

YP signs low in the seat so she doesn't draw attention to our conversation. "Before Kyle, before Cheer, before you, I was B U S T E D."

"No shit?"

"And not by my dad, or principal. Real, real B U S T E D. They————my room, took————everything."

"That's why your room is so empty!" She must have been doing some really serious art to get the cops to raid her room. If the thought of a raid at the moment wasn't so terrifying, I would be impressed.

"Never————replace any of it."

"Did they . . . ?" I pantomime handcuffs, grab invisible bars in front of my face.

"Nah, in the end they not P R O V E it. And they not P R O V E this, either." She reaches out and squeezes my hand.

Fem Cop is holding up the mop marker, examining it from different angles, shoulder crunched against her radio, probably relaying a description. Big Cop stands to the side, looking more punchable than ever, copying info from our IDs onto yellow slips of paper.

"I tried. I tried telling you at the water tower," I start. How do I explain this to her? She's calm, I'm a mess. She's not going to want to stop. Why should she?

"What?" she asks.

"I can't keep doing this." I point around the car. "I can't keep lying to Mee and Ma; I can't risk getting kicked out of another school. Especially not now."

"There——-other schools."

"None with you in them."

We both cry, holding each other's hands. We almost laugh, until we remember where we are.

The cops, each taking a side, open the doors of the cruiser and order us out. They lead us around to the front of the vehicle. "Tilt your heads back," Big Cop barks, and motions for my benefit. We comply. Fem Cop takes a flashlight off her belt. *What are they doing?* They wouldn't give me paper, but they wouldn't . . . beat us or anything, would they? Fem Cop clicks on the flashlight and shines it up my nose. *What the fuck?*

She does the same to YP and shakes her head no to Big Cop. His shoulders drop in disappointment. He hands back our IDs, along with the yellow slips he was writing on earlier. "We took——all——information so————you—-get away——-————," he says to YP. Fem Cop makes a show of keeping my mop. *Great.* She can have it.

"—-——free to go?" YP asks. Big Cop dejectedly tells her yes. YP grabs me by the arm and leads me away. Thank you, Universe.

276

. . .

We bike around Sunnyside, me standing on her back pegs. She pedals steadily. We're taking the longest and windingest path back to Lee. Don't want the cops knowing my car, my plates, or where I live. We take our time.

"Want to eat?" she asks at a red light. My stomach has barely settled from our near-arrest, but if YP wants to eat, I'm not going to say no. We lock her bike outside of a place called Tofu and Noodles. We sit at the table in the window so YP can keep an eye on her wheels. The waitress pours us waters and sets out five tiny bowls, each with a different type of kimchi.

"Kimchi smells like S O C K S," I whine.

"It's good!" She fills up a chopstickful and hurries it into her mouth. We pore through the pictures on the menu. I'm only halfway present. The other half of me is still in the back of that cruiser, headed for a holding cell.

"What you want?" YP flips through the menu.

"Split this with me?" I point, and her eyes light up.

"My favorite!" YP smiles, tapping her chin. She tells the waitress our order and eats more mouthfuls of kimchi cucumbers and kimchi classic. I still don't have an appetite.

"Why aren't you freaking out?" I ask her. I can't stop bobbing my knee up and down. I tap the table with the white plastic chopsticks. YP reaches over and stops my hand.

"It's over, we're fine," she signs with one hand. It's amazing how far her sign language has come. We haven't had our phones out since 5 Pointz, and we haven't missed a beat.

"Well, I'm freaking out." I start bouncing both my knees.

"I see that." YP takes her hand back so she can eat some more kimchi.

"What are we going to do, though?" I can't stop looking back over my shoulder, at her bike, still locked to a street sign, but no one is coming. We should be fine, but I don't feel it yet.

"First, we eat. Then, bike to L E E. Then—"

"No, about us. About . . ." I mime spraying paint across the air.

"Oh, I don't know," she says, forgetting to sign, mouth full. I'll never eat kimchi, never.

"Stop, right? Shouldn't we stop?" My right hand chops my left palm. "Why didn't you stop when you got caught?"

"I did. For a long time. I was done. I was out."

"What happened?" I'm rapt, still. On the edge of my seat, and she practically spits out her soda, laughing at me. "What?" I shake my hands furiously.

"I saw your whale and I couldn't help myself." She almost looks bashful, breaking eye contact and looking down at the table. Our waitress brings over a huge plate, steam rising off of the whole grilled octopus that we ordered. She takes out a pair of scissors from her apron and cuts it up for us before leaving us to it. It smells and looks delicious, and suddenly, finally, I'm starving.

We pop the front wheel off YP's bike and angle the body into the back of my car. I'll take her home eventually, but I'm not ready to let her go yet. She takes up her usual position, sitting back against the glove box, cross-legged in the passenger seat. I turn on Lee and crank the heat.

"Can I ask you a T O Y question?" I ask before pulling out.

"You're not T O Y."

"Why did that cop do that? With the flashlight?" I mime shining one.

"To see up your nose."

"For what? D R U G S?" This gets a big laugh. "Told you I'm a toy."

"That's why you wear the mask," she motions. "The paint—-stain——nose hairs."

"You're kidding, right?" I ask, and she crosses her heart with her pointer finger. I turn the key. YP reaches out and touches my arm.

"Hey, can I ask you a question?" We should probably stop asking if we can ask and just ask.

"Just ask from now on, OKOK?" I tell her, and she smiles.

"Why you call me YP?"

"Uh . . . Don't be mad, OKOK?"

"Never."

"Your pants."

"My pants?!"

"You always wear Y O G A pants, Yoga Pants, YP." I squint and look away without really looking away.

"Ha! I like it," she says. "I hate J E A N S. *Hate*."

"What'd they ever do to you?"

"Make me feel huge. Yoga pants don't really have numbered sizes."

"Do you want a new name?"

"Nope, never."

I start to drive, but somewhere along Queens Boulevard I decide we aren't going back to her house. Not yet.

We pull into the small parking lot next to the acupuncture shop as the streetlights flicker to life against a navy sky. I should text Mee.

JULIA: be home soon-ish. At the wall with YP.

MEE: :) :O :) YAY. See u soon my love.

"So," I ask YP, "what do you think?"

"Of what?" YP looks around the small parking lot, confused.

"The wall!" I spread my arms out, presenting it through the windshield.

"I think you were right."

"I want to, and I don't." I bite my lip, it's not fair. I don't want to force her to give up her game. That's her choice. I'm worried my wall is a poor substitute for the real thing.

"Same." YP's hand moves back and forth.

"You and me, *together,* it's next-level art."

"T R U T H," she spells with a pursed smile.

280

"Why do you love G R A F F so much?" I ask her. YP takes her time before answering. She looks up and down Mee's wall.

"I love making art you can't escape."

"Big." I grin.

"Yeah, big."

"Big like a whale. Big and beautiful."

"Yeah, big," she repeats.

"Big is best." I elbow her.

"Okay!" She lets out a laugh and rolls her eyes to the roof. We take some time to consider the wall and our future in front of us. I can still smell the paint in the air from our 5 Pointz piece, but I'm sure it's only in my head. It was magic, working alongside her instead of against her. The closest thing to telepathy I've experienced outside of my dreams. Sitting in the back of that cruiser, though, I never want to experience that again. Mee will be thrilled if we paint her wall, but I'm sure YP will think it's too easy.

"Would you still love it, if it was legal?" I break the silence.

"Maybe. I might miss the R I S K. But I wouldn't stop."

"If it's legal, are we posers?" I ask.

"You'll never be a poser. That underpass was the best thing ever."

"Then we can't quit," I say, determined.

"But what about—"

"Cops can't stop us from writing on our own wall."

By the time I drop YP off at her house, my stomach has unknotted itself. It's almost relief. *We're okay.* Yes, we're safe and free and clear. But we're okay. *Us.* We're going to be OKOK. And we get to keep painting. Bless Mee. It's not about the risk. It's about the art. I know YP and I could make something impressive without the pressure of cops breathing down our necks. I can only imagine.

I notice my backpack in the rearview and realize there are still a few kinks in my gut to work out. Katz. And Casey. Casey wasn't the most professional interpreter I've ever met, but is professional really what I want? At least she cares. It could be a little much, but that's nothing time couldn't fix. I should have cut her some slack.

I feel the worst about Katz. I burned him pretty bad. All he ever did was help me, include me, even when he couldn't. That illustrated album. *Jesus, Julia.* You were such a bitch. I have to fix this. I have to apologize.

Greenlawn Drugs is still open. I'm here for one thing, I just hope they have it. As I look up and down the aisles I consider the letter I'll write Casey. I'll grovel if I have to. She should get to come back. That is, if she wants to. If I were her, I'd be through with me.

I zero in on a big bucket of sidewalk chalk. Perfect. I toss it on the passenger seat and rifle through all the papers on the car floor. All I need now is the yellow envelope that had my Bob Dylan album in it. The lyrics are all here, but I hope the envelope didn't get dumped out of my bag back in Queens.

My phone buzzes in my pocket: Ma checking in. My new rule is always answer their texts. I've put them through enough, and they only know the half of it. I'd like to keep it that way. I let Ma know where I'm at and my ETA, and she seems satisfied, even a little cheery. I crouch down and feel around under the seat, find a crumpled take-out bag. I reach in again and I'm in luck, there it is.

I bet Katz didn't realize his address was on the front when he gave it to me, reusing the envelope from some other package. Just what I needed. I tear off down the street in Lee, chalk safe beside me.

Mr. Katz lives in a big farmhouse. Smoke rises up from his chimney; he must be home. There are lights on, but they're all on the opposite side of the house. It's only chalk, right? I cut the headlights and pull over behind a big fir tree. Lee's gray paint job camouflages her well. After grabbing the bucket of chalk and the sketchbook full of signs, I close the door as quietly as possible.

His driveway is long, his house set far off the main road. At the end of the driveway, in front of the house, are two cars: his and Casey's. Ooh-la-la. I think fast, changing up my plans now that I know she's here. Nothing drastic, though. Still going for it.

I carefully pick out colors of chalk by the light of my phone. Despite the size of the bucket, the shades are limited. They're all washed-out pastel blue, green, pink, or orange. I'll make it work.

This'll be my first—and last—chalk piece ever. *Why can't you be more like paint?* I try my usual outlining method, and it works all right. But only all right. I'm going for *epic apology* here, and *all right-looking* pisses me off.

I push through, filling in the shapes, getting chalk fingerprints all over everything, mostly my clothes. Strange that the legal stuff is twice as messy. Takes twice as long, too. I really want to cover the driveway, but if I did, it would take until first period tomorrow.

The last orange stick wears down to a pebble and I pack it in.

I take out Katz's sketchbook, the one I illustrated all the signs in, and go to leave it in his mailbox on my way out. Unfortunately, his mailbox is attached to his house, right next to the door. But I just bombed 5 Pointz. I can sneak a book in a mailbox.

I creep up the steps slowly, hoping that the old wood isn't groaning under me. When I reach the top, the porch lights flick on. I dash to the mailbox as quickly as I can and try to fit the sketchbook in the slot. My hands are trembling and I accidentally drop the book. As I'm picking it up, I feel the door swing open.

"What are you doing here?!" Casey signs from the doorway. She wraps a blanket around her shoulders, covering up her matching pajama set. She's obviously pissed, but she looks

so dorky I can't help but smile. "You've caused me enough trouble. Go home." I stop her from swinging the screen door shut. I angle myself so she's looking at me and not my chalk masterpiece in the driveway. Let her see that in the morning.

"Wait! No. I—I wanted to say I'm sorry," I tell her. Casey looks over her shoulder into the house.

"Well, he's sleeping, so tell him at school."

"Not to him, to you." She's surprised to hear me say it and I feel so guilty for it. She never expected an apology from me, and not because she doesn't deserve one. She really, really does. I look down at the sketchbook I made for Katz and realize it shouldn't be for him. Of course it should be hers. "Hang on," I sign, and she wraps the blanket tighter, covering her arms while she doesn't have to speak.

I take out a pen from my pocket and uncap it with my teeth. I open up the book to two blank pages, and on the first I scribble out the sign for the word *sorry*. Then I draw her name sign, the one she's wanted since the day we met. I hope she understands. I hope she likes what I've chosen. I think it suits her.

"Here. For you." I hand her the sketchbook. She flips through every page, the blanket resting on her shoulders like a cape. When she gets to the last two pages, she looks up and signs,

"Forgiven."

$$(/\!/\!/ \; \breve{} \; \smile \; \breve{} \; /\!/\!/)$$

The kitchen light is on when I get home. I debate getting back into Lee and driving around the block until it goes dark. I don't really have a curfew, more like an unspoken rule that I should be home before midnight. I have three minutes. I park in the driveway. It's not like Ma will know what I've been up to.

But Ma isn't in the kitchen having her usual late-night Sleepytime tea fix. It's Mee, surrounded by tinfoil take-out containers. The whole room smells of onion, garlic, and butter. With the smallest hint of garam masala.

"Want to share?" she asks, without looking up.

"Sure." I sit across from her and scoop some chicken makhani onto a slice of almost-stale naan. Mee is an expert at reheating food. Every time I try to reheat leftovers, they come out scalding, and I burn my tongue so badly I can barely taste the rest of the meal. Ma is useless at it too, but she has the opposite problem. Cold in the middle. Mee's technique, whatever it is, is foolproof. Every bite warm and perfect.

"Makhani is my favorite," I sign, and chew.

"I don't doubt it, you're practically made of the stuff." She smiles.

"What do you mean?"

"When I was pregnant, it's all I wanted to eat." Mee takes the tin of shrimp pakoras and dumps the remaining two onto my plate. She folds up the tin and tosses it into the recycling bin. "Your poor mother. I made her go out and get it for me all the time. Almost every day. Once, I made her go twice in one day. I swear Rajdhani's is still in business because of you. It's certainly not because of that guy who works there, the rude one?"

"Avi," I remind her.

"Right. I'm lucky I met your mom; she doesn't put up with any shit. Like you." She takes my empty plate away and I help her clean up the table.

"Mee." I stop her before she begins washing our dishes. "I'm going to start the mural. But I'm going to paint it with my friend from school."

Mee hugs me and lifts my feet an inch off the ground. She bounces in place without letting go. I try to sign to her, tell her to stop, but my arms are pinned to my sides, so I just give in. I feel her laughing, and everything about it comforts me.

"I'm sorry about this year," I tell her when she finally lets me go.

"You're sixteen. It's to be expected." She brushes my hair behind my shoulders. "When I was sixteen, I tried to take a train across the country to see Nirvana play in Seattle."

"You did what? How? When? Wait . . . what?" I follow her around the kitchen as she puts everything away.

"That's a story for another time." Mee flicks the lights off and then kisses her thumb and presses it to my forehead. "I love you."

"I love you, too."

X∩X

I would never have gone back. I would have left my job at Mickey D's without a second thought. But I left my black bag in my locker and I want it. I want to use the last of my overpass paint for our new piece. I want all of our histories, YP's and mine, tangled up together on the wall, our wall.

"Thank God, you're here." Jordyn rushes over to me as soon as I enter the locker room, her face slick with tears.

"What happened to you?"

"Donovan," she signs, sobbing. "He fucking dumped me, can you believe it?"

"Yes."

"Come on, Julia. I need you."

"Of course you do," I tell her with calm confidence. "This is what always happens. You only ever want me around when you need something."

"Don't be so dramatic." She wipes her face dry.

"You're the one crying over that loser with Mountain Dew breath," I joke, and she chuckles.

"What am I gonna do?" she asks, eyes fixed on the floor.

"I don't know."

"You're supposed to make me feel better."

"Why should I?" I actually want her to tell me. I wonder if she even realizes how hypocritical she's being.

"Because we were friends."

"Were we?"

"Sometimes." She almost looks embarrassed. Almost.

"That's not good enough anymore. I don't want sometimes friends."

"Right, you don't want any friends because you're too cool or whatever. You're better than friends."

"I'm not better than friends, I want *better friends*. I want friends who are all in, all the time. It can't just be all on your terms. You have to care, care about more than just yourself."

"This isn't about you! It's about Donovan breaking up with me for that über-bitch with the glasses."

"Look, you'll get over it." I wrap my arm around her shoulder. "You always do. This isn't the first time this has happened, and it won't be the last." I open my locker and grab my black bag. I stuff whatever is left behind in the front pocket. Jordyn calms down, she pulls her hair up, ready to start her shift.

"You're right," she says.

"And when it does happen again"—I stop and look directly into her eyes; I need her to understand me—"I don't want to hear about it." I fling my bag over my shoulder and head out the back door. She stomps her foot over and over, and I turn around.

"Wait! Where are you going?" she pleads, eyebrows arched.

"I quit."

(ˆ ˆ) 人 (ˆ ˆ)

It will be the biggest piece we've ever done. Bigger than the underpass, bigger than 5 Pointz. We're going to have to work our asses off. YP hauls paint from my trunk while I lay out some tarps. It feels strange to be setting up properly, in the light of day. I've seen two cop cars pass us, and each time I swear I froze in place. They didn't give us a second glance.

YP's dad brought over two ladders this morning and now he's at breakfast with my parents. They seem to be getting along, even though he's probably the worst texter I've ever met in my life. I finish with the tarps and back up, trying to take it all in. A blue mote of plastic underneath our White Dove wall.

"Do you think we got enough purple?" YP asks, signs springing from her fingertips.

"Are you kidding? We probably got too much." We did go overboard buying the paint. Our parents pitched in, and it was so much easier without all the covert ops that we ended up buying enough paint for two murals.

I wrench open the small can of Clear Skies, a light blue color we're going to use to outline the mural with. It's light enough that it won't show through the finished piece. YP brings over some brushes.

"You have the paper, right?" I ask her.

"Paper? For what?" Her eyebrows angle together. Even her

facial expressions are getting better. She's losing her hearie accent.

"Our plans! The plans for the wall?" YP pats her pants out of instinct, I guess, because I don't know what pair of yoga pants has pockets. Her hands shoot up to her mouth, she's panicked.

"Oh, my God, I can't believe I forgot it. We can start tomorrow, I'm so sorry. Julia. Please, you have to—"

I hold my hands up to stop her. "Don't worry about it." I try to calm her down.

"Are you sure? What do you want to do? Should we wait, you want to drive to Greenlawn?"

"Whoa, whoa. Okay, deep breath." I take one for myself and mime for her to do the same. She does, but she still looks uneasy. "We don't need the plans, we've gone over it a dozen times."

"You want to start anyway?"

"Why the hell not? Since when do either of us carry around cheat sheets?"

"True."

"So chill. We got this." I dip both of our brushes into the paint and swirl them around. I look up at YP; a smile creeps over her face as she looks at our wall. She's ready. I stick out one of the brushes, a bead of Clear Skies drips over both our shoes.

"It's only the beginning."

ACKNOWLEDGMENTS

I have more people to thank than stars in the sky, and every last one of them makes my universe brighter.

Huge thanks to my team at Knopf. Thanks to Marisa Di-Novis for the tour and her contagious enthusiasm for books. To Ray Shappell for helping me design the heck out of my color-bombed cover; Stephanie Moss, who laid out the pages with great finesse and care; and, of course, my brilliant editor, Stephen Brown, who knows just how to make my stories shine. This book is beautiful because of all of you.

Thanks to everyone at my wonderful agency, Triada US. To Uwe Stender for his constant encouragement, and my dear agent, Brent Taylor, whose unfailing optimism and fierceness never cease to amaze me. Thank you for being my champion, agent, and friend.

To all of my d/Deaf, Hard of Hearing, and interpreter sensitivity readers, who helped make Julia's life and experiences as truthful as possible. Kelsey Young, Brook Wayne, Kimberly Bull, and Kate Boyd—thank you for your insight, honesty, and understanding. Very special thanks to Kalen Feeney, my wonderful ASL tutor and mentor in Deaf culture. I love chatting with you until my fingers hurt. If Julia ever makes it to the big screen, you're writing the script.

Nisha Sharma for your notes and enthusiasm for Julia's heritage and love of makhani.

Thanks to Jen at *Pop! Goes the Reader* for my gorgeous cover reveal.

My first-ever critique partners, Kiersi Burkhart and Cynthia McGean. Thank you for pushing me to get words on the page week after week.

To everyone who keeps me going through countless chats, DMs, and texts: Jon & Vicky, Blair, Brooks, Lygia, Nita, Summer, and Kaitlyn. To Taryn, who had milk shakes with me on the day we sold the book. And especially Fred, who sent me the nicest email I've ever received.

To Mr. Nick Maravell, greatest art teacher of all time. Thank you for getting me through high school and inspiring me even now.

To my two perfect pugs, especially Gouda, who doesn't know what a book is or how to read, but has had such an impact on my life, I must include his fuzzy face.

Grandma Pat, who always encouraged me to sing as loud as possible, and Grandma Alice, who wanted me to be quiet and read more books. You both shaped me in very deep and obvious ways.

Mom, thank you for letting me paint all over my bedroom walls and encouraging me to keep painting everything around us. Aunt Linny, thank you for inspiring me to create beauty out of the ordinary. You're the strongest women I know.

I consider Best Friend to be a tier, not a person, and I'm so lucky to have three incredible best friends.

Arielle Gardner, my sister and my first-ever BFF. There are pieces of you in everything I've written. Some more obvious than others. Thank you for sharing all of your stories with me, and keeping thousands of my secrets. I love you.

Cara Hallowell. For all the Fridays in comic shops and Collage. For knitting and puzzle games and podcast recaps. For baking obscene amounts of cookies in your perfect tiny kitchen. Now that we've met, I can't imagine Portland without you. Thank you.

Brie Spangler. You've been my sister-in-arms through our publishing journey. I don't think I would be writing novels if it wasn't for your encouragement to break out of comic panels. Meeting you was one of the best things about moving to Portland. One of the best things, period. Hand in hand into the void. Thank you for believing.

This book is for you, Roger. But you know that. Thank you for investing in my dreams, in me, in our little life together. I promise it's only going to keep getting better. I love you more.

Thank you, Universe.